IT COUl

HAPPEN IN

Oxford

Book 1

Turl Street Storytellers

EDITED BY
SARA BANERJI

Disclaimer

It Could Only Happen in Oxford is fiction. Although it is based on many well-known, and less well-known, places and events around Oxford, any reference to living individuals is accidental.

Turl Street Storytellers
7 London Place, Oxford OX4 1BD

Typeset by Anne Joshua, Oxford
Printed and bound by
TJI Digital, Padstow, Cornwall

Turl Street Storytellers

The Turl Street Storytellers is the collective name for some current and recent members of Sara Banerji's courses in creative writing, and publication of this little book is entirely due to her inspiration and infectious enthusiasm. The following have contributed to *It Could Only Happen in Oxford, Book 1*:

Sabita Banerji

Sabita Banerji was born in India and now lives in East Oxford with her daughter. She published her first novel, 'Kundalini Awake' in 2006 and has won Writers in Oxford, Oxford Editors and Writersdock writing competitions. Sabita has worked in international development for 15 years and before that worked with African, Caribbean and Indian dance companies.

Andrew Bax

Many years ago fate smiled on Andrew and allocated him to Oxford; more specifically to the attic above Robert Maxwell's bedroom in Headington Hill Hall. There he served a brief apprenticeship which was sufficient for him to make a career in publishing and, eventually, to form his own company.

Janet Bolam

As a child, Janet filled many school exercise books with stories about astronauts and life on distant planets. This gave way to frankly embarrassing adolescent poetry that petered out as the rest of life as a working mother took over. Now, with a career in the public sector behind her, she has picked up on her early interests, hopefully with more grounded results!

Vicky Mancuso Brehm

Born in Canada and raised in Brazil and Italy, Vicky Mancuso Brehm studied Geography at Hertford College. She works as a researcher in international development, and lives near Oxford with her husband and two children. And she did once work as a tour guide taking unsuspecting tourists on gruelling itineraries around European cities.

Jenny Burrage

Jenny's main claim to fame is that she could read the newspaper when she was four years old. She has been enjoying reading and writing ever since.

Kathleen Daly

Kathleen fell in love with medieval manuscripts at an exhibition in Rouen before she went to Oxford University to study history. She is fascinated by medieval ideas about the past, and has published a book, and articles in French and English, on medieval texts and manuscripts.

S. A. Edwards

S. A. Edwards was born in Blackpool, the child of a circus contortionist and an amateur fire-eater. A reclusive, auto didact artist and writer, S. A. Edwards has contributed to the

Reader's Digest *Guide to Great Britain*. An enthusiastic chicken keeper, S. A. Edwards lives in Blewbury, Oxfordshire.

Julie Farnworth

Julie has worked as a writer and editor since graduating with an English and History degree. Her creative writing has been published in *Mslexia*, and she has been shortlisted for a Fish award and the Apprentices in Fiction scheme. She has completed two creative writing courses at Oxford University's department for continuing education.

Wendy Greenberg

Wendy has lived in Oxford for 20 years. She has worked in bookselling and publishing in London and Oxford. She loves warm blue skies and, if granted one wish it would be to never have to wear a coat again! Her ambition has always been to be a doo-wap singer but time may be running out . . .

Neil Hancox

Having written many papers and reports when he worked as a physicist and materials scientist, Neil Hancox decided that the truth could be improved with a dash of fiction. So when he retired he started writing short stories. His work has been featured in several anthologies and he has performed at the Oxford fringe.

Sheila Johnson

An interest in family history prompted Sheila to enrol on a life writing course in 2006. To improve her writing skills she joined

Sara Banerji's creative writing course in 2007. Seduced by Sara's enthusiasm she now writes short stories and is working on her first novel.

Kamini Khanduri

Kamini lives in Oxford (where she was born) with her husband and two daughters. She works as an editor at a book publishing company. When she's not at work, she enjoys doing crosswords, eating in nice restaurants, talking to her friends, going to the seaside, and watching Dr Who.

Keith McClellan

A retired Oxfordshire head teacher, Keith had a successful play published by Longmans in Kenya, and articles published in the *Times Educational Supplement* and the *Oxford Times*. He contributed to 'Inside Lives' on Radio Oxford, and has had various short stories published in the Aynho Writers publications. He has written for, directed and performed in the last three Oxfringe Festivals.

Lesley Maile

Lesley lives thirty miles from Oxford, her favourite city, which she visits regularly to meet with fellow writers. When not writing, leaving out the dull bits, she enjoys her garden and plays clarinet.

Nichola May

Nichola has lived in Oxford for 21 years. She home educates her three children and is passionate about autonomous learning for all ages. A slave to multi-tasking she has been known to knit through funerals, and usually writes in the kitchen while eating chocolate chips and baking chocolate chip-less cookies.

Isobel Miller

Isobel's writing is a form of escapism. She loves to transform various subjects into fictional stories trying out different genres and enjoys rising to challenges. She finds writing a chance to express her thoughts and some experiences in her life.

Jackie Vickers

Jackie has tried her hand at many things over the years, from being an architectural assistant to University teaching. Writing has now taken over her life and she frequently finds her fictional worlds preferable to the real one. She is writing her first novel.

Sara Banerji

Sara Banerji is the daughter of Anita Mostyn, a novelist who wrote in the 1950s under the pen name Anne Mary Fielding and of Sir Basil Mostyn, 13th Baronet of Mostyn. She is descended from the family of Henry Fielding, the 18th century author of *The History of Tom Jones – a Foundling.*

Born in England and evacuated to various large and crumbling country mansions during the war, Sara spent the later part of her childhood in a mud rondavel in what was then Rhodesia, where her father grew tobacco. She later hitchhiked round Europe, worked as an au pair and went to art school in Austria.

While working in a coffee bar in Oxford, Sara met her husband to be, a law undergraduate from India. She lived for seventeen years with her husband and three daughters on tea plantations in the Nilgri Hills of South India and Assam in the North East. At one stage, they tried setting up a dairy farm in her husband's ancestral village in West Bengal, but were defeated by a combination of economic and political turmoil and ferocious monsoons.

During these years she also held exhibitions of her oil paintings, rode as a jockey, and started writing novels.

Returning to England, broke because of the prevailing currency export laws, she found various creative ways of supplementing the family fortunes such as buying ponies and giving riding lessons, cooking Indian feasts for people's dinner parties, and setting up a gardening business. Her first novel, *Cobwebwalking*, was published at around this time.

She now lives in Oxford where she continues to write, paint and make her unique papier maché and wire sculptures, teaches writing and cultivates her prolific allotment.

Cecily's Fund

Cecily's Fund

*Profits from this publication are being donated to
Cecily's Fund*

Cecily's Fund was set up in 1998 in memory of Cecily
Eastwood of Stonesfield in West Oxfordshire, who died in
an accident while volunteering with orphans in Zambia.
Still based in Oxfordshire, the charity now enables almost
10,000 Zambian children and young people, who have
been orphaned or made vulnerable by AIDS, to go to
school and college.

Their small UK team works through well-run Zambian
partner organisations to buy and distribute shoes, uni-
forms, books and pens and contribute towards school fees,
to children who would otherwise have no hope of going to
school. Education is one of the most effective ways of
protecting children from HIV. Cecily's Fund commits to
supporting them right through to the end of school, and
also offers some of them the opportunity to train as

teachers or as peer health educators, running school work-shops on HIV. Cecily's Fund staff and trustees regularly visit Zambia to ensure all donations are being spent effect-ively exactly where they are needed, and it has twice won award for the clarity and transparency of its annual reports.

For more information see www.cecilysfund.org

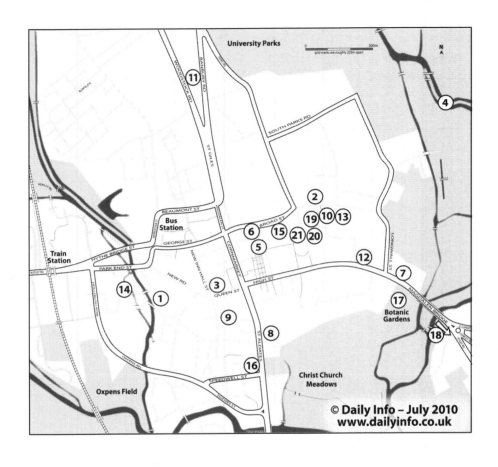

© Daily Info – July 2010
www.dailyinfo.co.uk

Contents

Introduction

With a group of local Oxford authors, Sara Banerji has created a guide book of stories, sad and happy, scary and violent, ghostly and romantic. The stories are all set in unusual places in and around the city. Each delightful story is followed by a short factual description of the story's venue. Read the story, find the place in which the story is set on the map and you will see amazing artefacts, learn about forgotten events of history, and discover new and off-the-beaten-track places. You will be led to parts of Oxford that few people know about, you will discover another side of Oxford that you did not know existed.

1

Down, Deeper and Down

LESLEY MAILE

It must have been five or maybe six hours ago when we stood discussing our finances outside Malmaison.

Time wise, I cannot be more precise because from this position I am unable to consult my Casio. If my guess is correct, as I stare up at the barred windows, dawn is just around the corner. They say things appear better in the morning, but I have my doubts.

If only I could turn the clock back to when my little bundle of five-foot deliciousness dithered, trembling and apprehensive, whilst I coaxed her towards unquestionably the most salubrious hotel in Oxford. 'Look, My Sweet, our money is as good as any sod's', I said.

The trouble was, our garb, outdated and Oxfam tainted, fell short of the mark. However, I refused to allow scruffy cuffs to spoil our planned celebration of love. I told her she looked like an off-white angel.

When I originally heard about Hotel Malmaison, the ex-prison, I wanted to visit it straight away, but My Sweet, not always compliant, objected.

'But Malmaison is different,' I said. 'It's a prison that takes no prisoners – I gotta see those cells all tarted up – and I especially want to see the one that isn't.'

My Sweet had one of her long faces on, 'Prison visits with you crying "Get me outta here!" was enough clink for me,' she said.

She does exaggerate, she only came to see me once.

It took a few days cajoling, but in the end she agreed to spend our anniversary at Malmaison.

Although she still had reservations. 'I ain't stopping in no cell overnight,' she said.

'At those prices! No chance of that,' I said, 'unless they're giving a room free with every drink.'

Ha! The irony.

I gave her a cuddle and told her my plan. 'First off, we'll go to the bar and have a drink, and then we can go deeper down and have a poke about.'

She shrugged me off. 'You're a pig for punishment,' she said, 'all sorts of evils lurk in those vaults – if you want to go down, then you go down alone – I'll guard the drinks.' Occasionally, she can be negative.

So, that was the agreement. I pulled on Malmaison's

glass doors and a smartly dressed man pushed his way in front. His Adam's apple pressed against a fat, knotted, fleur-de-lis tie.

'Sincerely sorry,' he said and entered, cocky, with his bird.

We lingered in the lobby and My Sweet said it was a shame I didn't have something fancy like that hanging round my neck. She was right, with an old school tie you can get away with murder. Often rejected, we understood the significance of the symbolic uniform. Ours stated loser. She tugged at my shirt collar trying to bend the upturned corners flat and I remember thinking, as I stared into her scalp, that I might nip to the jeweller before the night was out and get her an engagement ring. Cursed toughened glass and metal shutters make the task nigh on impossible for a lightweight like me, but I was prepared to have a go if I could find a crowbar, so that shows you the depth of my love.

While I stood uncomfortably suffering the attentions of my intended – she had moved on to spitting on her sleeve in order to rub a stain from the front of my shirt – I became conscious of the error of my ways. It was earlier in the day, along Dead Man's Walk, when I waylaid a random stranger for a fraction of the contents of his wallet. I had briefly thought I might persuade him to hand over his navy silk tie too, but he was a reasonable sort and prepared to part with his money so readily that a twinge of compassion came upon me. Shame, the tie would have covered the grease spot nicely.

Anyway, after the spit and polish, My Sweet and I ventured towards the stairs leading to the bar, whereupon I hesitated and suggested a couple of six packs from the offy in Walton Street might be a safer bet. She, now inside, had grown confident and was having none of it. She shoved me forward. I didn't protest.

We have been together a year to the day, and from day one I learned the powerful intensity of true lovemaking. Before she happened along, I had to pay for *it*, and was badly in danger of catching *something*, if you know what I mean. You could say she saved my soul, my life. Now I'm clean living, albeit in a grimy sort of way. I owed her a fancy drink at the least. She was going to have a cocktail made from a mixture of every type of alcohol, all topped off with a glacé cherry on a stick. And for me, a double brandy in an over-large glass, allowing me to swish, with vigour, the miniscule droplets around the base just like my Uncle Joe used to do at Christmas when I was a kid. He'd agitate the brandy and puff on a cigar and not go near either again until the next Christmas. He used to say, that way the treat stayed special. My Sweet had never been in contact with a glacé cherry on a stick, so I realised just what a special treat this was going to be for her. I suggested, if money to spare, we share a cigar in loving memory of Uncle Joe, but My Sweet preferred to share a sandwich in loving memory of her overweight mother.

Normally we would row about such a thing, but harmony was the word, at least until the night was out. It would have been nice to compromise. Compromise is a true sign of oneness, but a cigar sandwich would have been stupid.

We went down the black, carpeted stairs and before we arrived at the bottom, I ran my hands through my hair and wished that I had fleeced our benefactor for his comb. That's the trouble, I'm too bloody soft; if a nice person mugs you, be assured, it'll be me.

We walked towards the bar, I whistled nonchalantly. My Sweet started to giggle. She was in danger of ruining it, and I told her so. She said something about being deliriously happy.

Ahhhh.

While waiting to be served, we looked at a display of photographs, glossy magazine quality, with the caption: *VENTURE FURTHER DOWN AND ENJOY A NIGHT IN ONE OF OUR SUPER SLINKY CELLS.* And a dog-eared black and white photograph of a cell in its raw state, bare walls, barred windows and iron bed, invited – *STEP INTO THE SHOWROOM – IF YOU DARE.*

'I dare,' I said, 'I bloody dare, I've done the real thing, that's just pretend.'

My Sweet went up close to the old photograph and said coldly, 'But once upon a time it was real, very real.'

I shuddered.

I ordered the drinks and the barman, who I reckoned from the fall of his lips did not want to serve us, said, 'All told, it'll be eleven quid.'

And I said, *'Eleven flipping quid.* How much minus the cherry?'

He said the cherry was free. My love-bitten heart sank. I'd ruined our special day. I reflected back to earlier. I should not have let my muggee off so light. When I'd pushed him up against the old city wall – not too roughly mind – and demanded he show me the colour of his money, I noticed he'd got a newly minted twenty. I didn't want to wipe him out so I said a tenner would do. See what I mean? I'm an all-right bloke.

So there I was, leaning on the bar kicking myself, when a voice from behind said, 'I'll get this round my friend.'

I turned slowly towards the person purporting to be my friend. His features were vaguely familiar. He told me we had met around noon in Dead Man's Walk, by the old city wall, and was ten pounds lighter for the experience. 'Make that brandy a treble,' he said.

I'd heard of turn the other cheek, but this show was stretching it surely. Not that I said anything, after all I didn't want him to change his shout to 'POLICE'!

The three of us sat in a cosy corner together and unbelievably My Sweet started to flirt with our newfound friend. I was a bit upset by that but not wanting to muddy the ambience I didn't let it show and any rate I was feeling pretty mellow after knocking back the golden fire water. It was smooth, slid down easy, like a herring down a guillemot's gullet. Down deeper and down it went – this put me at a disadvantage.

Once, when I was a nipper, we were all sitting around the turkey and a cracker went bang. Startled, I dropped a dollop of jelly onto my lap. Uncle Joe picked up his over-sized glass, took a swig and said, 'Pay attention, little soldier, always be *on guard*'.

Best advice I ever had and throughout life I have adhered to it, but a treble brandy annihilates *on guard*, nothing stands to attention after a few trebles I can tell you.

The brandies kept on coming, loosening my tongue and I told our magnanimous friend how, if he had not been such a nice victim, I would have had the entire contents of his wallet. I poked his chest and said, 'And your tie.' I was a bit aggressive, but he just laughed.

Guess what he did next. He took it off! Tied it neatly around my neck, winked, and said, 'It looks better on you than me – and besides I've got a lot of ties.'

By the look on My Sweet's face I think she was falling in love with such goodness, tell you the truth, so was I. In fact, I was a bit choked – couldn't speak – words failed me. I patted him on the shoulder. He smiled at us, said we could stop the night right there in Malmaison, in his room, said he had a few loose ends to tie up and didn't need it that particular night.

'Save you having to stagger home,' he said.

That is when she opened her big mouth, 'We ain't got no 'ome.' The times I've told her not to tell it like it is. To save face, I was about to decline the offer. Then I remembered that I had not yet ventured down the iron treads and I felt myself being enticed, especially when he said the bed was a double-sprung, four poster with knobs on.

Having imbibed a bucketful of cocktails, My Sweet seemed to have dispelled all fears about going down. She led the way and she told him I was interested in taking a peek at the unadulterated cell.

He said, 'Go ahead – why don't you.'

It was an odd feeling, when I stepped in. Miserable in its

starkness, it brought back bad memories. Unnerved, I wobbled a bit and then thought, 'Hey, what the hell, this time I can just walk straight out,' and that is what I went to do when I felt a blow to the back of my head.

I am awake now, stretched out on this metal un-sprung prison bed. And hell, I cannot move a muscle. My right wrist is tied to the bed with a pink silk tie – and my left wrist the same only with a red silk tie. A green silk tie tethers my right ankle and an orange silk tie secures the left. He was right he has a lotta ties. The navy stripe is still around my neck and getting tighter by the second and I wonder, as I sink down, deeper and down, where is My Sweet Anniversary Girl.

THE GRIZZLY END

Robert d'Oilly began building Oxford Castle in 1071. By 1230 it was partly used as a prison, and continued to be until 1996. MWB plc bought it and turned it into Hotel Malmaison. The doors opened in 2005. The metal stairs leading up to the open galleries remain, and one cell has been left untouched; the only thing in there is an iron bed.

2

The Road Not Taken

JACKIE VICKERS

I love everything about this place.

I love its modest classical exterior, its peaceful, unassuming interior.

I once heard a tourist complain that this building was uninteresting. 'Compare this with the elaborate church interiors of the same period in Bavaria,' he said crossly to his companion, 'or the beautiful ornamentation of the French or Italian Baroque. There is nothing to look at here.'

You have missed the point, I wanted to say. You mistake simplicity for plain-ness.

Every year I buy my season ticket for the Sunday morning *Coffee Concerts*. The music is always wonderful, but I also enjoy the historic associations, for the Holywell Music Room was the first purpose-built concert hall in Europe and is still in continuous use for recitals and concerts.

But is there more to my attachment to this building than Sunday music in an historic venue? Of course there is.

This Sunday, for the first time, I have brought my young daughter, who already shows promise on the violin. As we are early, I tell her some of the history of this place and that gentlemen were asked not to bring their dogs into the concerts here. I tell her about the uproar when the leader's violin was broken by an orange, thrown with force from the audience. She is excited and full of questions. Then the rustling and whispering stops and is followed by a murmur of disappointment at the announcement that the soloist has been taken ill, and there will be a few changes to the programme. The replacement emerges from the door behind us and comes forward, smiling, to acknowledge the applause and I am deafened by the roaring in my ears from my own heartbeats. The performer steps back and leans over her violin for a final tuning. Her thick dark red hair hangs over her face as she adjusts the pegs, then she flicks her hair back and fiddles with the scarf she wears under her violin in place of a shoulder rest. After a short pause, she draws the bow across the strings with a graceful arm movement. And the first notes of the Bach B minor sonata fill the room.

Fleur Fleming looks exactly as I remember her, though her playing has acquired more emotional depth in the last fifteen years. When the applause for the Bach dies away she announces the first programme change and I now know that she has seen me, for it is the Telemann E minor sonata. And I am immediately transported to that terrible afternoon in my rooms and the last time she had played this piece for me.

We had met the summer before I came up to Oxford. To read music. I was queuing for a Prom ticket, outside the Albert Hall, when Fleur fell over my feet. That's all it takes, one small collision to alter the course of a life.

The first thing I noticed was her long red hair, then her graceful movements and laughing green eyes.

She said the first thing she noticed about me was my feet.

What do I remember about that first summer in London with Fleur? Certain moments stand out, the steady ominous pulse of the slow movement of Beethoven's Seventh on our first date at the Festival Hall. The sweet melancholy flute melody of Gluck's 'Dance of the Blessed Spirits' at a lunch-time recital at St Martin in the Fields. A military band playing in the park as we sheltered under trees during a shower. But of the things that mattered the most to me, only the taste of her skin and the memory of the weight of her hair in my hands, remains.

I remember her mounting excitement as October and

her second year at the Guildhall School of Music approached and my sadness at our unavoidable separation. She had heard there were to be staff changes, and spent feverish hours setting before me the relative reputations of the remaining teachers and what this might mean. In the end it was only rumour and she soon moved on to concerns about her violin and its possible shortcomings in the upper register. Difficult times, as I tried to calm her apprehensions and attend to my own. Then term started and we began, inevitably, to see less of each other, though we managed to meet most weekends. If a musical event was timetabled for a Saturday evening, Fleur would catch the last train, to be with me by midnight. We would get up late and race across the parks and up Holywell Street in time for a *Coffee Concert*. Later she would play her current studies to me, anything from Mozart to John Adams. She was already showing a preference for the Baroque and always ended with some Bach or Corelli, which I believed would be retained for ever in some storage facility of my mind. The holidays were long and we still managed afternoons on the river, picnics in the woods and music-making with our friends, but for Fleur, set on a performing career, there were also hours and hours of practice.

But I had assumed too much and when the hammer blow came it was far worse for being unexpected. We were walking back through the parks after our Sunday morning concert and I was talking about finals, which were only weeks away, when Fleur, who clearly had not heard a word, told me that she had been offered a place at the Juilliard School.

'New York!' I had said.

She was dancing with excitement. 'Think what it means!'

But I could only think that she had gone to New York for an audition and had never told me. I had become fixed on the how and the where, like someone who has just heard of their partner's infidelity and repeatedly returns to details of the time and the place.

For more than two years we had made music and made love and it often seemed like the same thing. I had been enchanted by her loveliness and her talent and it suddenly came to me that I had been drifting uncritically in her wake. And even then, despite this unwelcome discovery that her charisma cloaked a blazing determination, I could not really believe her ambition would destroy my dream of a steady job, a place in an orchestra for Fleur, and a modest house in a leafy road filled with children and music. But Fleur would have none of it. Nothing less than the world stage would do. We argued for hours. Fleur talked of the reputation of the Juilliard teachers, the standard of the other students and the guarantee of a future on the concert platform.

I disagreed. 'No-one can guarantee your future as a soloist.'

'America is the land of the possible.'

I remember pleading my own case, a contact already made with a music publisher.

'You expect me to give up my chance for your job. With a music publisher!' she said dismissively.

'You'd be happy playing from manuscript, I suppose.'

'Well, Bach managed!'

And so it went on all afternoon, from bad-tempered bickering to tears and shouting on her part and mutism on mine. In truth I would not give up the promise of a secure future in a city I loved, for an unknown number of years dancing attendance on Fleur. In the end there was no more to say. I think we both knew this was our last afternoon together and all our love and regret seemed encapsulated in her faultless rendering of our current favourite, the Telemann E minor sonata.

Why should this sorry tale be any different from any other love affair gone sour from a familiar mix of young love, immaturity, ambition and selfishness? Would a more determined or experienced couple have known how to negotiate those obstacles of time and place? She sent letters from America full of what I saw as facile declarations. Eventually I tied the letters up and hid them, with my memories, under my socks.

A small elbow nudges my arm and I join in the clapping. It is painful leaving my memories of the cluttered student room where I had lain on the rumpled sheets on our last afternoon, enveloped in the rise and fall of that Telemann sonata.

The room empties and now that I stand close to her I see there have been changes, after all. There are fine lines around her eyes and deeper ones by her mouth.

'A fine performance,' I say.

'Thank you. I had forgotten how good the acoustics are here.' The old energy and sparkle has diminished, she seems tired.

'You never came back to Oxford,' I say quietly, trying not to make it sound like an accusation.

'I heard you were married.'

Fleur stands at the back of the stage by her violin case and its precious contents, the Guarnerius loaned by the Guildhall, which she always keeps within reach. She slackens her bow and clips it into the case and I see there are no rings on her long slender fingers. The violin lies there, wrapped in the red silk scarf she still uses to protect her collar bone. I recognise it as my last gift to her.

'The colour hasn't faded,' I say, hoping to get beyond our cool meaningless exchanges.

'Some things don't'. She avoids my gaze and looks across to the entrance where my young daughter is eagerly sifting through CDs for sale.

I follow her glance. 'I don't think she'll find anything she doesn't already have. She's a great fan of your Baroque Ensemble. You have quite a reputation now,' I add, 'recitals, recordings, visiting professor at Milan . . .' and I realise, too late, that she will know now how closely I have followed her success.

She nods. 'Are *you* busy?'

I don't answer.

'Music publishing is satisfying?' she persists.

'The children are musical,' I say, to change the subject.

'Children?'

'My son shows promise on the keyboard. But he's young and still fidgets. I'll bring him next year.'

'And your wife?' Fleur snaps her case shut and zips up the outer cover. She turns, but I can't hold her gaze.

'She plays the oboe,' I say, deliberately misunderstanding.

Fleur looks at my child as she runs across waving a CD. There is an intensity to Fleur's expression that I have only seen once, on our last afternoon together, when she spoke of the Juilliard, and her future.

'I hear you play the violin too.' She leans forward. 'What's your name?'

I draw my daughter towards me and hold her closely.

'Fleur,' I say, 'her name is Fleur.'

The Holywell Music Room, built in 1742, is the oldest purpose-built music room in Europe and therefore England's first concert hall. Many musicians, including Haydn, have performed here. Coffee Concerts, established more than twenty years ago, are held here nearly every Sunday morning in addition to regular concerts and occasional free lunch-time recitals.

3

Tiger Lily

Thomas Madison Browning had long intended to give up smoking, but women – or rather one woman – was making it impossible.

Every Friday, after filing papers in his briefcase, he would stroll out to savor the two loves of his life: Cohiba Exquisito cigars and the woman who sold them.

He studied her hands, a ring on every finger, as she passed the cigars across the counter.

'Bells on her toes', Thomas said out loud.

'Sorry?'

'The rhyme, you know:

> *Ride-a-cock-horse to Banbury Cross,*
> *to see a fine lady upon a white horse,*
> *with rings on her fingers and bells on her toes,*
> *she shall have music wherever she goes.'*

19

She smiled. 'You're funny.'

Thomas had never been called funny before.

One Friday afternoon, as she served him, her blouse slipped and she revealed a shoulder. 'It's a tiger, can you tell?' she said. 'Had it done at the tattoo shop next door. I do so love a man with a tattoo.'

'A-a-a.' Thomas said, then closed his mouth and left without taking his change.

Thomas took Monday morning off work. He sat down among the nose rings, fluorescent hair spray, hookah pipes and leather corsets.

It was only a small design, a woman on a horse.

'I'd like a name on it,' Thomas said. The tattooist obliged. Thomas winced.

'Popular name,' said the tattooist, helping Thomas on with his shirt, 'you're the third bloke this week wanting that. If she's anything as great as my Lily, then good luck to you.'

'Your Lily?'

Tiger Lily is an alternative clothes store/piercing and tattoo studio based in New Inn Hall Street. Until 2010 the newsagents just around the corner in New Road sold cigars (including Cohiba Exquisito) from a humidor on their shop counter. 'Ride-a-Cock Horse' is a traditional nursery rhyme that originated in the nearby town of Banbury.

4

Oxclean Day

SARA BANERJI

Sometimes a whole day would go by and Maria would not talk to a single person. She had a little radio and that made things better. She would imagine that the people talking on it were addressing their words to her alone, and sometimes she would talk back to them – 'Oh yes, I do so agree with you', 'That is such a sensible suggestion' – that sort of thing. Nothing contentious. Perhaps if she learnt to be a bit more contentious, her life would not be so lonely. When she looked out of the window of her flat, she would envy the passing people because of the way they often talked and laughed with each other.

Because she lived alone, and did not have much money – only the minimum old age pension – she did not do much shopping. But whenever she did go to the supermarket, she always tried to have a little chat with someone there. Perhaps say a word or two to another shopper who was searching the same shelf: 'What lovely strawberries, don't you think?' Or, 'Don't you think these flowers are pretty?' She found that if she phrased her words as a question the other person would be compelled to say something back. If she just said, 'What lovely strawberries,' the other person might just nod before moving on. Of course she never bought extravagant things like that, but she loved looking at them.

So when there came a ring on her doorbell and it was not the postman asking her to keep a parcel for another flat – no one ever sent parcels to Maria – but a large middle-aged lady, Maria had to restrain herself from gabbling. She had a tendency to do this, conduct a sort of one-sided flow of conversation that lacked a pause moment during which the other person could get away. This time however, the other person started talking first.

'I'm Rose,' the woman said and smiled showing some large teeth. Maria was about to offer her own name in return but the woman did not give her a gap for it. 'As you probably know, next weekend is Oxclean.'

'Oxclean?' Maria looked blank.

The large woman called Rose looked irritated. 'All of us who live locally go out and clean the roads and parks. Pick up the filth left by those disgusting people who go around spitting, mugging people and overturning dustbins and riding their bikes on the pavement.'

23

'Ah,' said Maria, wanting to know how bikes on the pavement increased litter and hoping it would come out as the discussion progressed.

'So I wonder if you and your family would volunteer to join us,' said Rose.

'My son lives in America, I'm afraid,' said Maria. 'But I could do it.'

The woman surveyed Maria with a doubtful expression.

'I'm stronger than I look. I can still do things quite well in spite of this shaky thing,' said Maria hastily, taking hold of her hand. She added, a little wistfully, 'The only problem is, that I'm not very good at cleaning.' Her son had said once that the reason he did not come to stay was because his wife thought Maria's house was dirty.

'You wouldn't be on your own,' said Rose. 'You'd be paired with someone who knows the ropes. Safer like that, too, with hoodies around. Well?'

'Oh, yes,' said Maria.

'Well, there we are, then,' said Rose, patting Maria on the shoulder. 'Come round to my house, number fourteen, on Saturday morning.' Rose was gone before Maria could say another word.

The hours till Saturday passed very slowly. Maria wondered and wondered who her cleaning partner would be. All week she planned the things she would tell the other person. About how James, her son had just got a promotion. How her seven-year-old granddaughter was a wonderful piano player. How pretty Julie was, even though her front teeth were missing at the moment. Maria hadn't seen Julie in the flesh yet – the fare to the States was much too expensive – but James had sent his mother a recent photo.

Saturday arrived at last. Maria knocked on the door of number fourteen, and Rose came out, frowned, looked at her watch, and said 'I thought I said ten.'

'I lost my watch you see,' said Maria. 'It broke and I put it down and forgot and when I went back . . .'

'I'm not ready yet,' said Rose. 'Go home and make yourself a cup if tea or something. Come back at ten.'

Maria tried to do what Rose suggested, but her hand was shaking too much to accurately pour the kettle and so in the end she just sat down at the kitchen table and counted the minutes.

A quarter to ten came at last. She tried to make herself walk slowly so as not to be early this time.

Rose stood in her front garden, surrounded by plastic sacks, rubber gloves and nipper sticks. One other woman was there already.

Rose said, 'This is Lucy and this is – I'm sorry I've forgotten your name.'

'Maria,' said Maria.

'Hello, Maria,' said Lucy. She looked nice. Maria hoped that Lucy would be her partner. Maria and said to Lucy, 'Aren't these gloves lovely.'

Lucy looked surprised, gave a little giggle, and said, 'Yes.'

'I always think yellow is such a happy colour,' said Maria. 'Don't you?'

Lucy looked flustered and said, 'Yes' again.

'I used to have pair of gloves like this,' Maria went on, 'but they got a hole in them. You see I put them too near my . . .' But Lucy was no longer listening. Other people were arriving now and Lucy and Rose were greeting them.

Maria picked up a nipper stick and tried it out. 'Oh, isn't this wonderful,' she said joyfully to a man who had just arrived. 'Look how it opens and shuts, just like a little dragon's mouth – my name's Maria. Which colour are you going to have? Do you think the purple is the prettiest?' The man said, 'Bob. Yes, they're very clever,' and quickly turned to talk to someone else as though, Maria thought, he was escaping from something.

At last Rose began to give out the equipment and allot partners. Maria waited and waited, filled with joyous suspense, wondering who would be hers. People began gathering in twos, taking up their equipment and wandering off, chatting and laughing.

'And Maria and Jenny will work together,' said Rose. She looked round. 'Jenny? Jenny?'

'She's not here yet,' someone said.

'She insisted that she had Mesopotamia this year. You think she'd take the trouble to be on time.' Rose looked irritated. 'Oh well, Maria, start without her and I'll send her along to join you when she arrives.'

Maria looked alarmed. 'In Mesopotamia? It's a long way away.'

Rose's lips made a sort of snapping sound. She took a breath as though trying to calm herself and said, 'Off the Marston Road. Go past the new Islamic centre, then turn left. Lovely place. Long footpath between two branches of the river or canal or something. Hence the name. Lucky old you.'

Maria set off clutching her gloves, nipper stick and plastic bag. They were lovely things but she felt sad all the same. She cheered herself up with the thought that, soon Jenny would arrive. She reached the start of the lane and went down along the side of the Islamic centre. To her right was a playing field. The sound of men shouting came from it.

Straight away she saw a thrown chocolate paper and picked it up with her nipper stick. It was tricky because of the problem with her hands, but she managed finally. The stick worked beautifully. She wished there had been someone with her, to whom she could praise it. She wondered, as she dropped the paper into her plastic bag, if Jenny would come with her own nipper stick or she and Maria would have to share.

She carried on along the lane, poking into the grassy verges manipulating her nipper stick. Every time any one approached she looked round hopefully in case it was Jenny but it never was. She reached a bridge, where water dropped in a gentle slither onto the rushing foam below and stopped there for a while, leaning over the rail, breathing in the smell of river water and soothed by the sound of the waterfall.

A man went by and his dog stopped to make a mess. Maria waited till the man was out of sight, in case it embarrassed him, before trying to pick it up. It was much more difficult than bits of paper and old bottles, but Maria managed it in the end.

On the other side of the bridge, the path turned right. It was edged by verges of ancient trees and tall grass, beyond which on either side ran little rivers. A white plastic bag hung from a tree where the wind must have taken it but it was out of Maria's reach. A coke bottle floated in the water, but she could not reach that either.

Three boys went running by and Maria hoped they would drop something, but they didn't.

A baby in a pushchair dropped its dummy and Maria picked it up before the mother could and handed it over saying, 'Oh what a sweet baby. How old is he? How many teeth has he got? What's his name? Does he look more like you or his father?' The woman seemed quite keen to answer the questions at first, but after a while began to fidget and in the end went off with Maria's last question unanswered. Maria would never know if the baby had been like James and adored soft-boiled eggs.

Half an hour passed no one came. Not even Jenny. There were no houses in sight any more. No noise of traffic. Only the hum of water, bird song and the rustling of leaves. Maria began to feel nervous.

As she bent to retrieve a rusty tin, deep, old men's voices sounded from above. Maria leapt up, dropping the tin, and the couple of honking geese that had been flying over-head, landed elegantly on the water. Other geese were grazing on the rough field beyond.

She reached another bridge and dropped a stick in the water, then ran to the other side to see it coming out again. James had loved playing Pooh sticks when he was a little boy. But this stick did not come out again and Maria began to feel sad as well and afraid. By now she was tired but there still seemed an awful lot of lane to clean. She was reluctant to take a break and go home for lunch in case

Jenny arrived. She worked on for another hour, but still no Jenny. No one else came either.

She was teasing away at a stubborn bit of paper that had got lodged among the roots of an old oak, when she heard a step behind her.

She turned and was confronted with a young lad wearing a hood over his head.

Rose had talked about hoodies and muggings. Maria flinched in panic.

The lad came through the grass, and when he reached the path, leant against the trunk of a willow and nonchalantly pulled out a packet of cigarettes.

Maria held her breath but her heart would not stop racing.

The lad gnawed the cellophane off his packet off with his teeth, looked this way and that, as though challenging someone. Then going over to the canal, he spat the transparent crumple into it.

Maria gripped her nipper stick as the shining glint of litter began to weave and bob down stream. Looking at it spared her from looking at the youth, as though, by not seeing him he did not exist. When the bit of litter had vanished round the bend, Maria surreptitiously peeped up and down the lane, but no one was coming to rescue her.

The youth seemed to see Maria for the first time and to read her thoughts. He laughed and, keeping his eyes on

her, tossed a piece of paper from his packet onto the verge.
A little gust of wind took it and sent it fluttering onto a
clump of reeds growing out of the water. 'Go on. Pick it up
then,' said the youth.

Maria tried to speak but for a moment, as though her
throat had gone too tight and dry, no words would come
out. At last she said in a quavering voice, 'The trouble is,
I've got this bit of a shake you see, and I don't know if I can
manage that without falling into the water. What do you
think? Perhaps I could get into the water, but it does look a
bit deep, and – well, do you think because you are a young
man and strong that perhaps you would be able . . .' She
fell silent in a brief spasm of despair.

The youth was looking at her with an expression that
was half amazed and half amused. 'Wot you going on
about?' he said.

'You see I got all this rubbish up and Jenny never came
and I'm not very good at cleaning things and I did what I
could but I don't exactly think I could manage to get all
that out of the . . .'

The youth interrupted her. People kept doing that. He
pointed to the rubbish bag. 'What's all this then?'

'Rose gave it to me to put the rubbish in. But it's got
quite heavy now, and, you know, I'm getting a bit tired
and I'm not sure it . . .'

Slowly, and with his eyes on Maria all the time, the youth picked up Maria's rubbish bag and shook its contents onto the grass. 'There. It's lighter now,' said the youth, handing Maria the empty bag. 'I bet you can carry it now.'

Maria felt like crying. There came footsteps. The sound of whistling. Maria saw, through the trees, another hooded lad approaching. He held a bottle in his hand. 'So that's where you bloody got to, Bog,' he said. 'I've been looking all over.' He reached the place where Maria crouched, shivering in the grass and gesturing to her, asked, 'Wot's up with her, Bog?'

'Cleaning the river or something. What took you so long, Ant mate?'

'Don't you take that line with me, mate,' said Ant. 'I told you I couldn't find you. And it takes time, that's what. The woman was looking all the time. I nearly got copped.'

The words wandered vaguely round Maria's mind. The hammering of her heart was slowing but she felt dizzy.

'What's she done then?' asked Ant, nodding his head in Maria's direction before pulling off the bottle top and taking a swig. When he took his mouth away, his upper lip was foamed with white like the river.

Bog shrugged and touched his temple with his finger, then reached out for the bottle. 'Pass it over. Don't drink it all. Come on, mate, let's have it.'

Ant passed the bottle, wiped his mouth and said, 'And what's all this stuff doing?' He kicked at the contents of Maria's emptied-out litter bag with the toe of his trainer.

Bog shrugged again. 'I chucked it out.'

'Come on, Bog. What you done that for?'

'A bit of a laugh.'

Ant turned upon Maria, and asked her fiercely, 'Wot you done to get it?'

Maria cringed away from him and began stammering things about Rose and nipper sticks and the missing Jenny.

'What, you gone and killed Jenny?' Ant looked impressed. 'And they only gave you community service?'

Bog was looking impressed as well. 'How did you do it, Grandma?'

Maria did not know what the answer was so, for once, said nothing. She thought she might be going to faint. She tried to fight it off. So embarrassing, with these two young people present.

'Must have been poison. She don't look up to anything more,' Ant said.

The two of them nodded sagely as though they had stumbled upon an important truth.

'She's not dead. At least I don't think so . . .' Maria began. 'But of course she might be. You never know with all this traffic. And that would be so sad, because you know, even though she's not here, she might have been a really nice person. Well everyone's nice, really. I should think you are . . .'

'What the matter then?' a voice was asking. Maria opened her eyes and found she was leaning against the boy called Bog.

'She's knackered, that's wot,' said Ant. 'Here, have a swig.' He snatched the bottle from Bog and offered it to Maria. She hesitated, so he thrust it into her hand. 'Only lager. Nice and cold. Do you good.'

Cautiously Maria sipped. It was nice.

'Go, take a big swig,' urged Ant. 'Me and Bog 've both done community service.'

'We never killed anyone though,' said Bog.

'That's good,' said Maria. 'Because killing people isn't a nice thing to do, at all,' and she took a deep swig and felt her heart rate slowing, her trembling lessening.

Ant said, 'Let's pick this lot up, mate, then we'll take her to G and D's with us.'

'I shouldn't think she's got the money,' said Bog.

'Shouldn't think she eats much,' said Ant. 'We could afford her a burger or something.'

Through half-closed eyes Maria sipped the lager, and as the two boys gathered up the thrown litter, she told them about James, and Lucy, and how Rose had knocked on the door, and about the man with the dog's mess and the paper bag in the tree and the lovely flowers growing in Rose's garden, and how the lady in Tesco's had come out from behind her counter the week before and helped Maria pick up her dropped potatoes. And how the doctor had told her she needed a. . . .

And Ant told Bog, 'Fancy giving a job like this to an old grandma. They ought to be ashamed of themselves. It's like the Nazis it is. I'm going to tell my dad to write to the papers about it.'

And Maria wondered what G and D was and felt happy because she had stopped minding that Jenny had not come.

The name 'Mesopotamia' in Greek means 'between rivers'. Mesopotamia, Oxford, is a narrow island that forms part of University Parks. It lies between the upper and the lower levels of the River Cherwell.

The land was purchased by the University of Oxford between 1860 and 1865. A footpath, Mesopotamia Walk, laid out in 1865, runs along the centre of the spur to Kings Mill.

The Domesday Book records a water mill on this site and

milling continued until 1825. One level of the river was once a millstream. From 1943 attempts were made to introduce wild ducks and geese which at first proved fruitless due to the otter predation. Now, however, large flocks of geese can be seen grazing on the banks. Until 1926 a ferry operated from a point half way along the walk, but this has now been replaced by a foot bridge.

If Maria, in the story, had kept on walking, she would have come to the end of Mesopotamia, and reached a little park. This is Parson's Pleasure, where up till about 40 years ago men could swim naked in the river. If passing punts carried ladies, the ladies would have to get out and go round a fence to avoid the sight. Turn left and walk on again, and you reach the park. If you go through this lovely place, you reach North Oxford and will have passed from one end of Oxford to the other by waterways and gardens.

5

The Room of the Red Sofas

JENNY BURRAGE

Jessica headed for the tall building at the corner of Ship Street and Turl Street, pushing baby Karmen in her buggy towards the aptly named Corner Club. Although she often visited her husband there, she still hadn't decided how to describe the building's colour. Was it a shade of green, blue or grey? Whatever it was, it blended elegantly and gracefully into its surroundings.

She avoided the bikes leaning against it and took the buggy inside. Lifting Karmen gently so as not to wake her, she carried her up to the second floor, ordering a cappuccino on the way. The familiar room had a gilt-framed mirror and bookshelves on one wall and windows overlooking the street below on two sides.

She sat on the red sofa and gazed at sleeping Karmen. Her long dark lashes brushed against pearly peach cheeks. She was so beautiful and so small. Her tiny hands moved about jerkily as if in her dreams.

Eighteen months ago, sitting here on this very sofa, Jessica's life had changed. Her boyfriend Nicholas had suggested they have a meal here that evening. They had met outside.

They had been going out for a year and she had a very good feeling about the coming evening. He was late as usual but he gave her his customary peck on the cheek and looked her up and down.

'I've got something important to say to you,' he'd said. He added, 'You look nice, Jess.'

She was glad she'd worn the new blue strappy top with a touch of sequins and the highest of high heels. She followed him through the glass doors and up the stairs to a bar on the first floor, a large room decorated in cranberry and purple shades with low leather arm chairs scattered around even lower tables.

'Had a good day?' he asked.

'Yes it was really good, but maybe I was just happy at the thought of meeting you here tonight. It was a lovely surprise.' She squeezed his hand. He pulled it away and took a handful of peanuts. 'Cool!' he said.

In the restaurant, Nicholas recommended the seafood pasta and rocket salad.

'Sounds good to me.' Jessica fiddled with her watch strap.

The waiter took the order.

'I am Felipe,' he told them. 'I will be looking after you this evening.'

As they were eating, Jessica broke the silence.

'There's a new film with Kate Winslet on at the Phoenix. It's had really good reviews. Shall we go? I think it might be too late after the meal so maybe we could go tomorrow?'

'Can't tomorrow.' Nicholas passed her the garlic bread.

'Oh well never mind. Just a thought.' Jessica took the bread and pushed the pasta around her plate. She wasn't hungry. When was he going to tell her? She slipped off her shoes under the table and waggled her toes.

'What was it like at the bank today?' she asked. He frowned.

'People asking for loans. Us having to refuse. You know what it's like.'

The waiter approached.

'Dessert?' he asked. They both shook their heads.

Nicholas picked up the wine menu.

'A bottle of your best champagne please and could we have it upstairs?'

'The room of the red sofas, sir. Of course. I shall bring it to you there.' He winked at Jessica.

'The room of the red sofas, that's a lovely name,' she said. Upstairs they sat opposite each other on the velvety sofas.

'Wow! Champagne!' Jessica wondered if he'd got the ring with him or whether they would choose it together. She could hardly sit still.

The champagne arrived and Felipe opened it with a flourish and poured it out. He bowed and went to the couple sitting in the window to take their order.

Jessica's hand trembled as she tried to steady the glass to her lips. Still Nicholas didn't speak.

'What are we celebrating, Nick?' The words flew out of her mouth, she couldn't stop them.

'You've obviously guessed.' He smiled.

'Yes. I think I have.' Her heart beat faster as they clinked glasses.

Nicholas leaned forward as if he was about to kiss her but he didn't.

'I'm joining the army, leaving in two days time. It has to be goodbye.'

Jessica's thoughts splintered around her.

'What?'

'I'm sorry if this news has come as a shock.' He reached for her hand but she pulled it away.

'How long have you known?' She wanted to hit him.

'I applied months ago.'

'Why didn't you tell me before?' She could feel tears pricking at her eyelids.

40

'There was no point.'

'But why is it goodbye? Soldiers have wives don't they?'

'Wives?' He sounded startled. 'It wouldn't be fair to you. I don't want to take on the responsibility.'

Responsibility, that's how he sees me, she thought clenching her fists.

'We had a good time together. I never pretended there was more.' He seemed surprised she should think otherwise.

Something inside Jessica's head exploded and she got up and lurched towards the door sobbing. At that moment Felipe came in carrying a tray of glasses and wine and she collided with him. The two ended up in a heap on the ground among the shattered pieces of glass. The red wine was trickling along the wooden floor as they both sat dazed for a moment. Felipe jumped up and helped her to her feet leading her back to sit on the sofa.

'Are you all right?' he asked. She liked the way his dark hair flopped over the bluest of eyes.

'I think so.'

He retrieved her shoe, shook it to make sure there were no shards of glass in it, and put it back on her foot.

'It fits you, Cinderella,' he laughed.

Nicholas snorted but Jessica smiled through her tears.

'I'm so sorry. I'll leave my name and mobile number and

then I can pay for the damage.' Felipe handed her his ordering pad and she scribbled it down.

'I'll pay,' Nicholas said, 'it was my fault.'

'No thank you,' she said.

Next day Jessica got a text from Felipe asking her to call at the club that evening. She didn't want to go but she knew she must. The thought of going back to the place where she'd had that awful shock made her tremble. Anger? Yes, but the more she thought about it, Nicholas hadn't promised anything, had he? She had read too much into their relationship. Misery? Absolutely. 'Snap out of it,' she kept telling herself. She would text Nicholas and wish him good luck in his army career.

Her friends at work had wondered why her eyes were red and puffy and why she looked as if she'd just got out of bed. She felt slightly better after she'd admitted what was up. It was a relief to tell them.

'Now I've got to go back to the club and pay,' she told them.

'Bad luck, Jess!' they said, 'Hope it doesn't cost too much.'

That evening she made her way to the club. She had washed her face and applied some lip gloss and a touch of mascara so as not to look too devastated when she got there. As she reached the door she was tempted to turn round and go home, but then she saw Felipe through the glass doors. He waved and she had to go in.

'Hello, Cinderella,' he said. 'Come and sit down and have a drink. On the house of course.'

'No thanks,' she said. 'I have to go.' Was she imagining it or did those very blue eyes look sad when she refused? He was probably sweetening her up for the amount she was going to be charged. She fished in her handbag for her credit card and waved it at him.

'I'm so sorry about the trouble I caused last night. How much do I owe?'

'Nothing, mi amor.' He smiled. 'The club's insurance will settle all that. You do not have to pay. And besides we both tumbled together.'

'But why ask me to come here to tell me that?'

'Now it is my turn to be sorry for bringing you back, but really I am not sorry at all. I had to see you again.'

'Why?' She stared back at the blue eyes.

'Do you not know what a beautiful woman you are, Jessica? You see I learned your name from what you wrote on my notebook.'

'But . . .' She wasn't used to compliments. These Spaniards, she thought, all flatterers. All the same she needed a bit of cheering up.

He took her hand and kissed it. 'I want to take you on a

date. Your boyfriend, he is mad to let you go. I would like to get to know you. Please say yes.'

And that was it, the beginning of their relationship. Rebound? The girls at work wondered. At first it was, she had to admit, but as she got to know Felipe everything changed. She grew to love him, more than she realised she ever could love anyone. Their Majorcan wedding had been amazing. Was it really a year ago that she became Mrs. Jessica Diaz?

It was just at that moment that Karmen opened her eyes and gurgled at her mother. Felipe came in carrying a tray and placed it on the table between the two red sofas. The baby stretched out her arms to him and he picked her up and gently kissed her.

'My beautiful daughter,' he said.

Unfortunately the Corner Club in Turl Street was forced to close at the end of 2009 and the Turl Street Storytellers who met there regularly to write now meet at Malmaison. The Corner Club was on the corner of Ship Street and Turl Street. Jessica's life changed here.

6

Sky Light

JULIE FARNWORTH

I was looking for a piece by Purcell when I heard the whisperer. The voice was male, edgy.

'Excuse me.' I tapped the arm of the young girl at the till, the only other person I could see.

'Can you hear someone?'

She pulled one ear plug from her ear and swung it like old chewing gum around her finger. 'You wait for help. Manager back soon.'

I tried to ask if there was anyone else in the shop. She shrugged and raised her voice, repeating slowly to make sure I understood there was no one.

'Up here stupid. Look up.'

I glanced to see if the girl had heard, but she was still glaring at me. I could see nothing on the shop ceiling.

'Up, outside.'

The young girl tossed her black ponytail as I quickly

purchased the piece. My mother says I should not have played the violin; that I would have looked smaller behind a cello. No one hears me play now, so I do not disagree. The girl with the dark eyes returned to scrutinising a score which lay open on the counter – Paganini caprice No 24. Impressive.

How did I know the whisperer was talking to me? His slow handclap when the penny dropped confirmed it. Course he shouldn't have been able to clap, but then he shouldn't have been able to whisper. And I shouldn't have been able to stand naked on a roof top in the middle of a city without attracting attention – but then a roof top is more private than you might imagine. In fact, if you're going to take your clothes off, I highly recommend a roof top.

He'd almost gone hoarse, he said, trying to attract the attention of a violinist but I am attuned to whisperers. Here is some of what I hear, spoken quietly behind fringes and fingers.

'Shame.'

'She should stay home.'

'She would be so pretty.'

I pretend the children don't follow me, laughing. It is how I climb onto the roof so easily. No one I pass on the stairs believes I can squeeze through the tiny window that gives free access to my iron man.

I didn't take my clothes off that first time. We just stood side by side. On my next visit, he held my hand, my fingers soft in his. That's the thing about flesh; it is so much more yielding than iron. He says he likes the way it spills from my clothes, pouring like water from a punctured bag. I like the way he does not spill but brims over with pride. His hands take it easy by his sides and his expression is full of secrets; played out across the city beneath his gaze.

You could not have guessed by looking at him that anything was different that third time. He reached for my hand in the same way he always did and was unruffled as ever. He suggested we inch forward to sit on the edge of the roof. At first I didn't want to but he is so solid I find him difficult to resist. I removed my shoes and socks and let my feet hang over the corner. His legs stuck straight out and he giggled each time the breeze raced across his feet. He said it tickled and he clung to my hand willing it to stop and not wanting it to end all at the same time.

He said I should stand up and lean into the wind, said there was no point climbing on to a roof if you are not prepared for the whole top-of-the-world experience, so I stood with one hand on his shoulder as I removed first my trousers and then the rest of my clothes. He was pleased and stood beside me showing me how to inch my chest forward to catch the best of the draughts. Currents of air rose from the narrow street below, catching me full in the face and filling my mouth, so I could not speak. He moved behind me and took both my hands holding them in the air, as though we were on a fairground ride waiting for the car at the front of the big dipper to tip over the apex of the track and pitch into freefall. I could feel the weight of him at my back, nudging me forward until my toes clawed at the edge of the tiles. Standing to his full height, he held tightly and lifted me, the air rushing to my ears as I dangled weightless. With a great surge, he swung me to the east and on to his shoulders. He handed me my violin case as the thirteen male voices of the Sheldonian Emperors joined with the Muses on top of the Clarendon Building. The notes from the trumpeter soared unsullied into the still sky, conducted from the same rooftop but orchestrated by my warm-hearted friend.

I performed Purcell's *Te Deum in D major* in front of an audience. The music filled every nook, wheeling and circling above our heads, the mellifluous warmth of the countertenor – the bearded Emperor fifth from right – wrung with tenderness. Even the four women above Trinity College halted their debates of astronomy, theology, medicine and geometry to join in; though he told me later he had struggled to persuade them. At the end of Broad Street, the little elephant weathervane spun his rider round and round.

The 6ft nude statue, the work of celebrated Angel of the North artist Antony Gormley, sits on the roof of Blackwell's Art and Poster shop, in Broad Street. The half-tonne iron artwork was commissioned by Oxford University's Exeter College.

He is in the company of the nine Muses on top of the Clarendon Building, the four women statues, which stand upon the roof of Trinity College, the thirteen heads known as the Sheldonian Emperors and a small elephant weathervane at the end of Broad Street.

7

Love Me Do

WENDY GREENBERG

Jodie, an atheist, had been brought to this sanctified spot by both serendipity and despair. She stood by the small prayer board in Magdalen College chapel reading the handwritten notices pinned there.

> 'Please pray for those whose names are written here.
> Please date your request'
> *Please pray for those who are lost like me, may I find my*
>   *soul mate*
> *Please pray that that he is the right one for me*
> *Please pray that God will intervene and give me a*
>   *husband. . . .*

It seemed that the ubiquity of the quest for love was one area that united both town and gown.

She had fled from her house that morning after a bruising attempt to create an online dating profile with her friend Tess. Jodie's initial enthusiasm for the task had been quickly tempered after scanning through a host of registered users, trying to get a feel for how to market herself.

'Open Arms' called out with – just the best hugger
  and kisser
'Tattoo Man' banged his drum with – I'm waiting for
  you.
'Fil_ander' was . . . surprise, surprise after sensual
  adventures
'Master and Commander' was ready to take charge!

Jodie shuddered, in disbelief of the depths to which she had sunk to avoid another car-crash relationship. Now she was well out of her comfort zone in these sacred surroundings but she had not felt at ease in front of her monitor either. The infinite possibilities of the bulging dating sites felt a million miles away.

The chapel was deserted and a sense of peace descended on her. She adjusted to the subdued light and stepped across the large marble flagstones, imbibing the unfamiliar smell of tradition and establishment. The high vaulted ceiling and the colossal sepia toned stained glass windows gave her a momentary sense of space. She edged away from the door and sank into the dark seating which curved up to her shoulders, holding her in its wooden embrace. She stroked the smooth wood, heavy with the scent of beeswax, put her head in her hands and felt choked by tears again. She yearned for that certain someone to share her life but fishing on a website had felt degrading, Tess was probably right.

The online dating had all started well enough.

'How would you describe me Tess?'

'I would describe you as my adorable, impetuous, reliable but maverick friend who loves life and has made a lot of poor choices – but I am not sure that is what is required here.'

'We'll gloss over that . . . User name first – Out to lunch? Gone to seed? Last Chance Saloon?'

'No, No, Jodie, I think you may have to take a more positive approach . . . what about Stardust? . . .'

'Nah! Too hippy dippy . . .'

'Golden Girl?'

'Jesus, Tess, don't you remember that sit-com about those retired women called the Golden Girls? . . . What about something like Beating Heart (not dead yet), Open Book (the plot unfolds), or Sassy Girl (ready to snap up)?'

The cracked old board hanging beside the chapel door was covered with a confetti-like collection of small white notices, each sheet cut uniformly, each handwritten notice arranged with geometric precision. A pile of empty paper lay in wait on the table ready to pounce on the hopes and fears of this academic community. Jodie gathered up a couple of the empty white sheets and settled back into the musty atmosphere, chewing the end of her pen thoughtfully.

Jodie began to write. She felt hypocritical and out of place in these surreal surroundings but there did not seem to be anything to lose in using this spiritual forum and its congregation to help her along her way.

Her arrival in the college had been unplanned; rushing out after her row with Tess, she had slipped through the entrance to avoid another confrontation with her ex-brother-in-law who she had spotted on the High Street. The elderly college retainer casually took her entrance money, raised his eyes from the racing pages and directed her out into the quadrangle. Inside, her sore eyes widened, it was breathtaking, the old cobbles, the honey stonework, manicured lawn and the opulent wisteria twisting and climbing from perfectly dug beds to delicately fringe the mullioned windows with clusters of pale mauve petals. She followed the path to her right and joined the shady southern cloisters. It led her into the chapel through a doorway beneath the muniment tower.

In here, time stood still, the air felt weighty, distant

whisperings of traffic and college activity barely register-ing. White petals fell on to the memorial stones from a carefully arranged display. She could not keep running from her demons. She had such high hopes earlier when she thought that shopping for love online might help her avoid her usual unsavoury choices.

As she scribbled furiously the tears returned and blotted out her words. She crumpled the paper, hurled another wasted dream to the ground and picked up another pristine sheet. She stared at it, unable to write.

She wrapped her arms around herself and massaged her hairline. A man entered, gliding through the chapel, his robes brushing the marble floor. He nodded his head toward the altar before progressing towards the prayer board. Under the watchful stony eyes of griffins, dragons and angels Jodie shrank yet deeper into the shadows.

The man's head turned from left to right as he scruti-nised the prayer board. Jodie's heart raced hoping he would move on but he lingered, still reading. A group of tourists entered and the man stopped reading and turned to them. Jodie willed him to move away but he turned back to the board and bent down. He picked up her discarded prayer from the floor. He placed it carefully on the table and very gently opened it, caressing its wrinkles back to its original form. He lifted the notice, read her words and nodded his head. She hoped the ground would swallow her. When it didn't, she opened her clenched fists and swollen eyes and raised her face. A knowing, baffled look met her gaze. A chord stirred within her and the anger and hopelessness that had unexpectedly brought her to this place of solace dissolved and she smiled. Halleluiah!

Magdalen College chapel can be accessed by visiting Magdalen College, High Street, Oxford. Whilst the college itself was built on this site in 1467, work on the chapel began in 1474 but the marble floor and bronze lectern are all that survive in the chapel from the seventeenth century restoration.

8

Buckland and the Elephant

S. A. EDWARDS

A handbill found crumpled on the floor of the Eagle and Child:

Bostock and Wombwell's Beast Show

Amongst the Number of Natural Curiosities arrived in this City, there seems none to equal or rival the wonderful elephant Esmerelda. Those Ladies and Gentlemen who have already seen this extraordinary pachyderm, are so highly gratified with the sight, that the Proprietor flatters himself, from their high recommendation that all ranks of people will gratify their curiosity, as she is undoubtedly the only one of her kind ever exhibited in the kingdom alive.

To be seen at St Giles Fair, St Giles Oxford
September 1st 1845.

'Roll up, roll up. For only three pence you can see her enormous ears, gaze into her ancient eyes and for an extra penny you can feed her a bun. Imagine, Ladies and Gentlemen, the sensation of her trunk as she takes the bun from your fingers. Dare you Sir?'

Mr Bostock the joint owner of Bostock and Wombwell's Beast Show was working the crowd. Inside the stiflingly hot canvas awning, Esmerelda the elephant swayed from side to side. The crowd queued patiently, waiting to be ushered in for their audience with the animal. The canvas flaps were lifted and they moved into the gloom of the tent.

'Cor she stinks. Take a whiff of that, Ma,' shrieked a small ginger-haired boy as Esmerelda lifted her tail and defecated.

'That's a massive one. Your dad would only need one of those for the whole allotment,' observed the child's mother.

'Go on then, mate. I'll give you a penny to feed it,' shouted a young man egged on to bravery by his girlfriend.

The elephant raised her sad eyes and with infinite gentleness took the bun from his outstretched hand. She waved the bun above the heads of the crowd before twisting her trunk and popping the bun into her mouth. The crowd roared with laughter.

'Me next, me next,' called the ginger-haired boy, elbowing his way to the front of the bun queue.

The Very Reverend William Buckland, Canon of Christ Church observed to his wife that he had rung three times and no tea had yet arrived.

'It's that blasted Fair,' she replied. 'The maid has the day off to go gallivanting. I'll fetch your tea'. She stumbled over the tortoise as she left the room.

Dr Buckland's study contained almost as many live specimens as dead ones. The tortoise lived under the sideboard. A ring-necked parakeet sat on a stand by the window. A gecko rolled its eyes from a glass tank. Every surface of Buckland's study was covered in shells, bones, fossils, minerals, stones, books and half eaten bits of toast. In the centre of this organised chaos sat Dr Buckland with an enormous ginger cat on his knee. His black ecclesiastical robes gave him the appearance of a necromancer. He rubbed the cat affectionately under the chin and it blinked its green eyes at him in appreciation.

'The Fair' he mused to the cat 'I haven't been for years. I think I would like to go.' The cat feigned interest then looked disgruntled as it was pitched off his knee.

Dr Buckland was a zoophagist. His ambition was to eat his way, for scientific research, through the animal kingdom. While younger men were arguing about Darwin's new theories of evolution, Buckland was eating his way through bluebottles, crocodiles, moles, bats, beetles.

He had started his hobby by trying to eat his way through the animal world in alphabetical order. When aardvark proved too difficult to source he decided to eat what came available and simply to chart his progress through the different species, sub-species and genera, with tasting notes. His rooms in Christ Church were decorated with the skeletal remains of his most interesting meals, mounted in life-like poses.

'We'll move her after dark,' said Mr Bostock. 'I don't want no one getting a look at her for free'.

The elephant's chain was unbolted from its stake and with sharp pokes behind her ears to encourage her, she was walked across the town to the Christ Church meadows where the rest of the Beast Show was camped. The animal moved slowly and shook her head from side to side.

'She don't look well, Boss' said one of the coster-mongers.

A jet of green, stinking faeces exploded from her and spattered all over Mr Bostock's trousers.

'Shit' he said.

As the sun rose over the Isis and the mist of morning evaporated away, Esmerelda the elephant died.

Dr Buckland whistled as he walked to the Beast Show camp. The rat tucked inside his hassock fidgeted and stuck its nose out of the vestments to see where they were. 'Stop that! It tickles,' The Very Reverend remonstrated. 'Excuse me young man, I would like to see the elephant.'

'Miss, if you don't mind' said Consuela, the Bearded Lady, 'Better ask the boss, that's him over there. I don't know how much he's going to charge to see a dead one. Can't imagine there's going to be much demand myself.'

Buckland's heart missed a beat.

'Dead?' He almost sprinted over to Mr Bostock. 'When did it die?' he asked.

'Bloody hell. Have you come to give it the Last Rites?' said Mr Bostock.

'No, no, no. I would like to buy the carcass,' said Buckland.

Mr Bostock stopped looking depressed and started to look shifty.

'Well, that's a very valuable bit of meat, that is. How much is it worth to you?'

Buckland threw caution to the wind and said with great aplomb 'Three shillings and six pence.'

'You are taking the mickey, Reverend. I could feed the lions for a month on Esmerelda. I need at least ten guineas to make it worth my while.'

'I'll pay you eleven including delivery' said Buckland, who was warming to the art of negotiation.

There was a tricky moment as they negotiated the gate

into Tom Quad in Christ Church college, but with a lot of shoving and pushing, the late Esmerelda eventually popped like a cork out of a bottle on to the grass.

Now Buckland had his elephant, how was he to cook it? His scientific mind turned hypotheses and parameters, paradigms and conjectures till his synapses ached. If he was successful who would remember Darwin with his ridiculous new ideas? It would be Buckland's name that would echo down the ages. Cheered by this thought he set to work. So what to do? He wrote and drew till the cat thoroughly exasperated got off his knee and went to sit on its own, throwing him the occasional dirty look.

1. He could joint the carcass and cook it in pieces, but no, he knew the college butcher – Mr Grimshaw wouldn't have a chopper big enough.
2. He could wrap it in pastry. Elephant pie. He didn't like pie.
3. He could cover it in breadcrumbs. He didn't have a dish big enough to roll it in.

Buckland was beginning to feel dispirited.

'You could roast it' his wife suggested bringing him more tea and toast, 'but you will have to keep the meat moist. You don't want it to be tough. If I was you I'd stuff it.'

'What will I stuff it with?'

'Pigs' said Mrs Buckland who was a resourceful and imaginative cook 'and then you would have some extra meat in case there wasn't enough to go round.'

Buckland worked for two days non-stop until he had finished the masterpiece of his later life 'How to cook an elephant.' Extracts of which now follow:

i.   Dig a pit 12 feet square and 8 feet deep (in the middle of Tom Quad).
ii. Construct tunnels at each corner to act as chimneys with a turn spit/bellows arrangement at each tunnel mouth.
iii. Line bottom and sides with three feet of charcoal.
iv. Light charcoal with small pastilles. Insert prepared and oven-ready elephant.
v.   Pour gravel and top soil over elephant to seal.
vi. Keep fanning until the temperature reaches two hundred degrees Fahrenheit
vii. Cook for the required time and serve.

In calculating the cooking time (thirty one and a half hours) Buckland took the bold decision to ignore heat losses through the earth, including the sides and ends of the pit. He reasoned that heat would be conducted through the meat and it would heat up until an equilibrium state was reached, with as much heat being conducted through the meat as is lost to the earth, atmosphere etc. If the fire failed it might be possible that there would be insufficient heat to maintain the temperature of the meat at an adequate level but, he reasoned, some people may like their elephant rare. *Quod est demonstrandum* his feast would be ready on Thursday at 7.00pm.

Buckland, confident that his science would work, retired to bed.

'I'd like to see the look on Darwin's face when he hears about this,' he thought as sleep possessed him.

After morning prayers, Buckland with a supportive audience of Canons leaning from the windows of Tom Quad prepared for the mammoth task ahead of him. With the animal lying on her side he slowly paced across to the furthest wall of the quad, he turned and armed with a pike staff ran like the clappers towards the beast. There was a loud pop, as the pike staff punctured Esmerelda's stomach and she started to deflate like a balloon. There was a hiss as her intestinal gases started to escape and moments later a torrent of blood sprayed out of the wound, covering Dr Buckland from head to toe.

'I was not expecting that,' he told his appreciative audience.

Esmerelda's now flaccid belly was supported by two of the strongest kitchen porters. Buckland, still dripping blood, slit her from front to back and then poked a small scullery boy into the opening with the injunction to hold his nose. The boy, who was known universally afterwards as Stinker, rummaged around inside the carcass throwing out the vital organs to Buckland's waiting arms.

To Buckland's satisfaction he managed to stretch her intestines all around the quad perimeter and passing students had to step daintily over them. A pack of fox hounds appeared and were keen to help. Their baying and howling, the gagging noises from Stinker as he emerged from the carcass, and the buzz of the thousands of bluebottles all contributed to the carnival atmosphere.

When Dr Buckland opened Esmerelda's stomach he was interested to find an inordinate quantity of half digested buns, one pound, seven and sixpence in small change and a bunch of keys. He made a mental note to return the keys to Mr Bostock. The college cooks stepped forward. Esmerelda was stuffed with three pigs, each pig stuffed with a capon and each capon stuffed with sweet bay leaves, and the cavity was sewn shut. Ropes were attached front and back.

Buckland arranged his work force into two teams. One team was to balance the animal while the other team was to move her into the pit or 'Elephantarium fornax' as it was now called. After much heaving the elephant was rolled into her final resting place.

Esmerelda was cooked lying on her back with her legs in the air and with the tip of her trunk sticking out of the oven to act a pie funnel.

The fire burnt, the elephant cooked, the smell of roasting meat filled Oxford. An interested crowd gathered at the gate to the quad and jostled to peer in. The dons stood around occasionally fanning the flames with their gowns. The undergraduates larked and the Very Reverend Buckland sharpened his carving knife.

As the bell, Big Tom, brother to the more famous Ben, struck seven, the pit was opened and the elephant was revealed. The cooks tied ropes around her legs and dragged her up onto the remnants of the lawns where they started to carve her.

In Christ Church's ancient dining hall the tables were laid for the feast. The college's silver and crystal glinted in the candlelight. The blue-faced gargoyles stuck their red tongues out rudely at the proceedings. The only woman at the feast was Elizabeth I who looked down from her portrait hung above the High Table. She would have enjoyed the event, having the stomach of a king. The doors opened and in staggered the college porters carrying trestle tables loaded with mountains of meat. The meat itself was a rather alarming red. At the lectern to the side of the top table Buckland stood to read the Horace-inspired epigram he had composed in place of the college's normal grace:

Nunc est bibendum, nunc pede libero barrus pulsanda tellus.

This translates as 'Now is the time for drinking, now is the time to beat the earth with unfettered elephants' feet'.

He sat down pleased with himself. His fellow masters all applauded politely and then started a critical debate as to what he should have said – *barrus pulsanda* or *barrus pulsande*. The argument still runs to this day.

Esmerelda fed three hundred people with enough leftovers to keep the workhouse in broth for a month. Buckland was the first to be served. He piled his plate high as an encouragement to the others. He selected for himself the animal's tail as a particular delicacy. Esmerelda's trunk, a little charred on the outside was carved into pretty rings, like calamari. He had one of those as well. Cumberland sauce was served as an accompaniment. He had thought long and hard as to what beverages should accompany the meal. In the stygian darkness of the colleges wine cellar he had come across a box labelled 'Ritual Siberian Shaman Elixir.' This substance is made by Siberian shamans, who consume large quantities of the hallucinogenic fly agaric mushroom. The tribe wanting to share in the shaman's experience then drink his urine. These samples had been donated to the college in 1837 by Colonel FFyens Todgerington after his wife had mistakenly opened a bottle and given it to her bridge ladies.

'Just the thing' he said.

As the dark brown viscous liquid was poured into the masters' glasses the students looked quietly relieved that, through college funding cuts, they were limited to beer. It took the party nearly five hours to consume the meal. And what did it taste like? It was agreed by most people that it was an acquired taste. Buckland thought it tasted like crocodile.

Some of this story is true and the bits that aren't should be.

- *Esmerelda's skeleton can be found in the Oxford University Museum of Natural History.*
- *Scorch marks from the fire are visible on the front and rear legs. Close examination of the left hand femur shows what looks like marks from the carving knife.*
- *St Giles Fair takes place on the Monday and Tuesday following the first Sunday after St Giles Day in September each year.*

- *Christ Church is open throughout the year. Tom Quad is the main quad glimpsed from St Aldates. Esmerelda's pit is in the middle. DO NOT WALK ON THE GRASS.*
- *The Very Reverend William Buckland, Canon of Christ Church and Dean of Westminster was born in 1784 and died in 1849. His rooms were in Corpus Christi College.*

9

The Portrait

SHEILA JOHNSON

'Oh bugger,' thought Megan looking down at her tights. There was a large hole on one ankle and a ladder snaked its way up her leg. She'd have to get some new ones. Her yellow fairy skirt fashioned from an Oxfam purchase was too short to wear without them.

She needed to look her best. This was the opening night for the first exhibition since she landed her dream job. Well almost. Once she'd worked her way up from dogs-body to Director it would become her dream job.

Tonight Sebs had asked her to go to the gallery and let in other staff and the artists, till he arrived.

What if Kane Triller turned up to see his portrait, thought Megan, as she dashed into Marks and Spencer. She loved his music and had downloaded it all. Bev, his aunt, who cleaned the gallery, had got her a signed photograph. Although Bev called her nephew 'A right little tyke', he'd agreed to have his picture in the exhibition because she worked at the gallery.

Megan had put pink and purple stripes in the front of her red hair in case he showed.

'Bloody stupid' her mother said, when she saw them.

Megan returned to the gallery, unlocked the door and slipped back in with her new tights.

'Wait up,' a voice shouted as she relocked the door.

It was Dan Russell, Oxford's brightest new artist, main exhibitor. It was he who had painted the portrait of Kane Triller. Today Dan had tamed his long hair into a fat ponytail and his jeans and tee shirt looked as if, for once, they'd seen the inside of a washing machine.

'Thought I'd get here early, miss the screaming crowds,' he joked.

'Yeah . . .' before she could finish Dan pushed past her taking the steps two at a time and went into the gallery. 'Where's my frigging picture?' he shouted.

There was an empty space. The carefully placed lighting focused on white wall. Where was the almost life-sized interactive nude of Kane?

'It's here, it must be, I only went out for five minutes.' Megan's voice faltered.

'You're joking' he roared, the stud ring in his nose flipping up and down.

'The door was locked,' she stammered. 'It must have fallen down or something.'

'What something?'

'I'll look, I'll find it.' Megan shouted rushing into the gallery.

Crash went the music and the lights dimmed as Megan set off the interactive performance that was supposed to accompany the portrait. Kane Triller's latest hit blasted through the gallery as holograms of him performing twirled in two corners. Coloured lights flashed over the empty wall. Megan started feeling her way around the room, searching for the picture.

As the music stopped and the normal lights came on, Megan's hand made contact with a casting of Kane's manhood. It wobbled then slowly fell to the floor, pieces slithering across the concrete.

Dan stood open mouthed beside the console.

'You imbecile, do you know how long it took to get that casting?'

'Not long by its size,' snapped Megan. She picked up a few pieces. 'Perhaps we could stick it together,' she suggested. 'I think the main features are intact.'

'It's a work of art not a piece of Lego. And where's my picture? That's the most important thing.'

'I'll search the whole building. If I'm thorough I must find it' said Megan.

'I'll help. Try not to break anything else' said Dan in resigned tones.

The middle gallery was in darkness as Megan got out of the lift.

'Argh,' gasped Megan as hot smelly breath wafted into her face.

'What now?' Dan shouted from the stairs.

'Just put the lights on. I'd forgotten the animals.'

A herd of mythical beasts belched and farted swaying around them as Megan and Dan began to search for the picture. Megan was sure one bit her bottom as she scrabbled in their landscape or was it a pinch?

'It's not here. I know I left the door locked, honestly,' she said.

Dan was silent.

The light switch at the top and final gallery refused to work.

'It's OK, 'said Megan. 'We can still find it. It's got that little glow in the dark bit on the end . . .' Megan stopped. Of course he knew that, he'd made it. She wished he'd say something; maybe shout at her, the silence was unnerving.

'Shit,' she screamed as something clacked in her ear.

An unearthly screeching was followed by 'bloody hell' from Dan. They crashed backwards into each other.

'What is this, Dante's bedroom?' he asked. 'Come on it's not here. Is there anywhere else?'

'The café in the basement, it must be there.'

Megan ran for the stairs and all the way down to the basement. Puffing, she halted at the entrance and Dan cannoned into her. The cafe was bright and clean, but picture-less. Megan's shoulders drooped. This was her first job and soon Sebs would be telling her she was no longer required. Even worse Sebs might keep her on to tell visitors why the picture was missing.

A door slammed. Megan looked. Who was that? 'Bev what are you doing here?'

'Always do extra cleaning for opening nights. I like to have a bit of a look as well.'

'Have you seen anyone else in the gallery?' Megan asked cautiously.

'No, just you two'

'What about my picture?' shouted Dan.

'Yours is it? I put it in there with the rubbish' she pointed her head at the cleaning room. 'Should be ashamed of yourself. Doesn't do my nephew Kanie justice in the proper department if you know what I mean and as for glow in the dark.' She sniffed, pulled her coat tighter and left.

Dan was checking for damage before Bev had reached the stairs.

Megan held her breath.

'It looks fine, let's get it back in place' he smiled.

He looks quite nice when he smiles thought Megan.

Careful you don't bump into that swirl of wind going past in the street; it might be Roger Bannister running late when he was Master of Pembroke College. His sub four minute mile run in Oxford was a first when he achieved it in his younger days as a student.

Beware falling over small creatures with hairy feet; they may have escaped from JRR Tolkien's room. They could be hobbits leaving on their search for middle earth.

Don't swoon if you catch a slight waft of beer when looking at the art exhibits, you may not be imagining it. In some dark corner there could still be some left over from its former use as a brewery warehouse. Brewer Street is just around the corner, but who stored alcohol here? Morrells or Halls Breweries are likely, or maybe monks who were brewing in Oxford from as early as 1452.

Tea, not beer, was Samuel Johnson's preferred drink as he

worked hard on his book of English language. His large teapot still resides in Pembroke College. You too can enjoy some tea in the café of Modern Art Oxford.

10

Rapid Response

KEITH MCCLELLAN

The wind was strong that night. As Harry held his glass under the *Famous Grouse* optic for a nightcap, there came a bang on the bar window.

Muriel was gesturing vigorously and mouthing something.

All that fuss over a nightcap, he thought as he slid his whiskey behind the bar and went to open the door. She must have forgotten her handbag, he thought.

'Harry? Oh Harry, have the bar staff gone?' she threw herself into his arms.

'Can't this wait until we get home, Love? I wanted to check the new lad has put the guest beer on properly.'

'They're outside Harry, stealing the beer fest. Do something Harry,' she stood up still gripping his arm.

'Pull yourself together Muriel.'

'Three big hairy men are rolling the barrels down the

path. Call the police, Harry, call them now or we'll have no special beers for the festival. Listen!' she held up her hand, 'There, what did I tell you?'

The scrape and rumble of barrels being rolled over the cobbled path convinced him.

'I'll try this new Rapid Response Unit, supposed to be here in no time. What did I do with the number?' Harry scrabbled through papers behind the bar.

'The number's in your mobile phone.' Muriel shouted.

'Blasted technology,' Harry cursed, scrolling down his phonebook.

'Thank you for calling the Rapid Response Unit; your call may be recorded for training purposes. The Rapid Response Unit has been set up to respond immediately to an emergency. Many emergencies require the attendance of more than one service. Do not contact this service if you are not in an emergency situation. For non-emergencies please ring the service you require during office hours. You may face a fine of up to one hundred pounds if you misuse this service.'

'Excuse me but I do have an emergency. I'm calling from The Turf and some men are rolling out my barrels as we speak.'

'If you need the Fire Service press one, if you need an ambulance press two, if you are witnessing a terrorist attack press three, If you are involved in a traffic accident press four, if you are suffering a sexual assault press five, for any other violent crime press six. For all other emergencies press seven.' He pressed seven.

'Thank you for calling the Rapid Response Unit, our consultant will be with you shortly. You are currently, fourth in the queue.'

'What are you playing at, Harry? They're half way up Bath Place by now.'

'It's not as rapid as we thought, love, we're fourth . . . hang on.'

'Good morning sir, my name is Sharon, how can I help you?'

'Oh good morning Shirley, I'm calling from The Turf, some great hairy thieves are rolling out my barrels as we speak.'

'Sharon, sir, my name is Sharon, not Shirley.'

'Sorry, Shirl . . . er Sharon, I am calling from The Turf . . .'

'Tell them to send someone for goodness sake, Harry,' Muriel sounded desperate.

'Rolling out the barrels, you say? Can you explain that please sir?'

'I'm at The Turf, it's our annual festival tomorrow, or it was until this lot turned up.'

'The Turf, you say? Is this a betting shop? It's rather

late to be there at this time of night, rolling out the barrel, isn't it?'

'I am not at a betting shop, Shirl . . . Sharon. Now could we get onto the rapid response bit do you think? It's over half an hour since I started this call. Do you want the post code?'

'It's OX1 3SU, Harry, shall I say it again?' Muriel called.

'Shhhh, Muriel, I can't hear what she's saying.'

'You do understand there are severe penalties for hoax calls to this service sir. Being drunk is not acceptable as an explanation.'

'Now listen to me Sharon, I am not drunk. I am responsible for organising a major beer festival starting tomorrow, and some thieving bast . . . naughty boys, have stolen the beer. It is in aluminium barrels and they just rolled one lot away. They'll be back for another lot in a minute.'

'Just a moment sir, I'm looking for "beer barrels, aluminium" on our priority list and it doesn't seem to be mentioned. I need to give it a priority code and I can't do that if it's not listed.'

'But these thieving b's have removed valuable items of property and are in the process of rolling them down Holywell Street. What's the code for that?'

'We have to be more precise than that sir, or it throws out the monthly statistical return. Hold on a moment while I consult my supervisor. I won't keep you long sir.'

'Are they sending someone, Harry? What's going on? I think those men are coming back.'

'Are you there, sir? Well our supervisor has coded your incident as priority five sir.'

'What does that mean exactly? No, forget that, just tell me when someone will be here to catch the buggers.'

'May I remind you that this call is recorded sir? There should be someone there between the hours of three and five this morning. That is two to four hours sir. Thank you for calling the Rapid Response Unit. Have a nice day.'

Where is the tall slim, handcrafted yard of glass from which the world record was broken? Bob Hawke, former Australian prime minister quaffed a yard of ale in eleven seconds, to smash the Guinness World Record. Three pints of foaming beer gushing down his throat at less than four seconds a pint is some achievement, even for a prime minister.

When and where was Rhodes Scholar Bill Clinton sitting with his spliff, when he resisted the temptation to inhale? Was it on a Rhodes get together on a Turf Tuesday in the Hillary Term perhaps?

A much loved tavern with foundations dating back to the thirteenth century, served the slum dwellers in their ramshackle buildings on the outside of the old city wall which runs along one side of the building. Here, their unlawful activities were free from the jurisdiction of the governing bodies of the local colleges. The low beamed bar added in the seventeenth century, made The Spotted Cow a popular haunt. Gambling of various sorts had become so prevalent by the early nineteenth century, and horse racing so popular, that in 1842 the tavern changed its name and became 'The Turf'.

This well hidden inn can be approached through Bath Place, a narrow cobbled alley, opposite the Holywell Music Room. The sudden sharp turns and angles an indication of the original ramshackle cottages, now attractively refurbished.

Alternatively approaching from New College Lane, passing under the Bridge of Sighs and turning into St Helen's Passage, known at the time as Hell Passage, you pass the birthplace of the most famous of the slum dwellers. Jane Burden, wife of William Morris, and lover of Rossetti, was born here in 1839. She was the daughter of a stableman, and the family moved frequently from one dwelling to another in the Holywell Yards. She gave 65, Holywell as her residence at her marriage in 1859.

In recent years the October Beer Fest has offered a range of more than thirty cask ales to sample.

11

Blind Date

WENDY GREENBERG

Relaxation came easy at The Old Parsonage. Lucy eased herself into the soft armchair. The walls were Russian red and covered with eclectic portraits and cartoons.

The divorce had been taking its toll and she was at last ready to put Freddie behind her. Would she recognise her 'strong but soft' blind date? As she studied the menu and ordered the Very High Tea as they had arranged online, he walked in through the seventeenth century entrance porch.

'And you must be . . .'

Lucy glimpsed the red rose before his voice tailed off. She raised her eyes and they met Freddie's.

Enjoy the best afternoon tea at The Old Parsonage Hotel. The building dates back to Cromwell's time and is located in central Oxford between Keble and Somerville Colleges.

12

Just Another Tuesday

ANDREW BAX

As Joyce waited for the bus there was nothing to warn her that this Tuesday would be different. Off and on for nearly 60 years, she and Mildred had met for elevenses and always on a Tuesday. It was a routine that suited them both; apart from that and a shared interest in needlework, they had little in common. They had been friends at school and when they went their separate ways prim, beautiful Mildred, groomed for marriage by her ambitious parents, was sent to finishing school. On her return she promptly fell for an austere young man of lofty intellect who eventually became Wilsonian Professor of Byzantine Art at Pembroke College. Dumpy little Joyce had become a clerical assistant for the council and married into trade. Her husband was a butcher and they lived above the shop in Walton Street. She had only moved after his recent death and because of the surprising discovery that she had become the owner of five houses and three race horses. Yesterday, one of them had come in at five to one at Pontefract and she was bursting to tell Mildred about it.

Mildred, meanwhile, was waiting, wearily, for the bus at Rose Hill. The long walk from her retirement home, The Firs, had made her stiff. The Firs was a place of meagre comforts but it was all she could afford. She envied Joyce her four-room Abingdon Road apartment with a bus stop right outside, a live-in warden and an indoor swimming pool. When Mildred had heard about the swimming pool, envy had made her say crossly 'I've never heard anything so ridiculous. Who wants to swim at our time of life?' But she mustn't get cross she reminded herself. Although it was a struggle to get into town, she looked forward to these Tuesday meetings; they broke up the week and Joyce was a good listener. And this week, she had something exciting to tell her.

Joyce was the first to get to the Queen's Lane Coffee House and secured their usual table near the Ladies. Why hadn't Jimmy told her about the horses, she wondered. She knew he liked a little flutter – and why not? But then, they had never been short of money and she had always left that side of things to Jimmy. He was the business man after all and when he passed on – bless him – he left her very well provided for.

So when the trainer rang, the previous week, to suggest Mildred put a little bet on Port Meadow she had no hesitation in agreeing to £200. And she made a profit of £1000 – just like that!

Just then the door opened and Mildred weaved her way between the tables. Joyce smiled a welcome.

'You look happy' Mildred said.

'I am. And I'll tell you why.'

As Mildred listened to the Pontefract story she reflected on what she would do with £1000. It seemed a huge amount of money to her. She needed a new pair of shoes for a start. And it would be nice to go on a cruise. Somewhere exotic, like the Caribbean. Yes, the Caribbean would be nice. And then what about the children – and the grandchildren and, goodness, the great grandchildren! Suddenly £1000 didn't seem a lot of money after all. What would Joyce do with it, she wondered. Probably give it to the first Big Issue seller she saw. Mildred sighed.

'So I'm paying for elevenses today,' Joyce was saying. From the very beginning they had each paid their share because Mildred always had something rather plain, like shortbread, but Joyce could never resist a rich and creamy cake, which cost more.

'Joyce' she laughed 'There's no need for that.'

'Go on, let me pay just this once,' Joyce insisted.

Mildred sighed then smiled. 'All right, I'll celebrate your win with a little . . .' she looked at the display cabinet '. . . with a little carrot cake. And I have some exciting news about Edwin' she added.

Joyce settled herself for another long story about Mildred's talented family. Five children: they came popping out as regular as clockwork until Mildred began to look quite exhausted, poor dear. And as for Alexander – well! Thin as a stick and no conversation. Just shows you never know what goes on behind closed doors.

As Mildred recounted Edwin's life history, one she had told many times before, Joyce tried to remember who he was. One of the younger grandsons, she concluded, the one whose parents weren't married. Mildred had been terribly upset about them 'living in sin' until Edwin was born. Now they could do nothing wrong.

'And now' Mildred announced, 'he's been offered a place at Brookes.'

'That's nice, dear' said Joyce 'What will he be doing there?'

'Media studies' replied Mildred. She hoped Joyce wouldn't ask her what that meant because she didn't know herself.

'That sounds awfully modern.'

'It is. And Brookes has one of the best courses in the

country. Hundred of candidates apply, but they only take the cream.' Mildred knew she sounded smug but couldn't help it. 'And lots of good jobs afterwards' she added. Whatever it was, she was certain there were better prospects in media studies than in Byzantine art. Sometimes she felt a little bitter about the hand that fate had dealt her. Alexander had been so wrapped up in his work, writing books that nobody read, and poking about in dirty old monasteries that he seemed to forget about her for weeks on end. But at least she had the family.

'Such a shame you didn't have children, Joyce,' Mildred sighed, and not for the first time. And, as usual, Joyce replied 'But you've made up for both of us.' In fact, Joyce's only regret was that she and Jimmy didn't have children. He would have been a good dad, and with all the money he had been making, he would have given them a good start in life. Still, she smiled to herself, they had fun trying.

Theirs had been a marriage of harmonious contentment in which, as time passed, their separate lives merged into one. People were surprised at how well Joyce had adapted to being alone but in the dark, silent hours, she was grieving deeply. All she wanted was to join her Jimmy.

Now Mildred was talking about Jeremy. Was he the one in the BBC, or was that Rupert? Joyce tried to look interested but a sort of sizzling sound made it difficult to concentrate. More of a bubbling than a sizzling she decided, and leant forward to hear what Mildred was saying.

'. . . and do you know what? They said he couldn't come back unless . . .'

Joyce suddenly felt very, very tired. The bubbling had turned into a kind of popping. She closed her eyes.

'. . . they had to agree to that, of course . . .' The pops were getting louder. And then there was no sound at all.

'Joyce!' 'Joyce – are you all right?' No reply. 'Joyce!' Mildred almost shouted.

She gave Joyce's leg a little kick under the table. No response. She kicked again, harder this time. Nothing.

Shocked, frightened and confused, Mildred stared at her old friend, now leaning gently against the table, apparently asleep. Then, in a daze, she got up, waved vaguely to the waitress, and went home.

And Joyce went to join her Jimmy.

The Queen's Lane Coffee House is an excellent venue for snacks and light meals. There has been an Oxford eatery on this site for as long as anyone can remember – just next to the Palladian

extravagance of The Queen's College at the lower end of High Street, where it is at its widest. All the buses to and from Marston, Headington, Cowley and Rose Hill stop here – and the X13 from the Abingdon Road on its way to the John Radcliffe Hospital, which is the bus Joyce would have caught for her Tuesday elevenses with Mildred.

13

Deadly Sin

Isobel Miller

It is June and 28 degrees and I have finally arrived in the City of 'Dreaming Spires'. I walk under a bridge. My guide book says it is called the 'Bridge of Sighs'.

Two black-gowned men pass me. One is young with blonde hair, ruddy cheeks and a red carnation in his lapel. The other gentleman is older, maybe in his 50s, wearing a longer gown, he strides purposefully as they talk. Their voices are angry as though they are quarrelling.

The older man says, 'It is my duty to report you. Surely you can see that? There is nothing I can do to prevent your father from finding out. You should have thought of that earlier.'

The fair haired man says furiously, 'If you do, I promise you will regret it . . .'

I hear no more as they step through the college's ornate wooden doorway. The atmosphere becomes peaceful again. I can hear birds singing, bells ringing and music playing. What a strange country this is, so quiet and lonely. A motor cyclist passes me by but he is the only person on it. My dad has a motor bike. He drove, me behind clutching him and my sister behind me and baby Ranjit, lying across Mum's lap. My grandma sat on the back, elegantly side saddle in her pink sequined sari.

I step inside and there is a man standing at a door by a wooden book stand. Later I learn this place is called the Porters' Lodge. The disagreeing men are already there talking to this man. The pale haired man is looking very cross.

'Evening Robin, can we have the key to the Bell Tower?' says the older man. I think he is trying to ignore the younger man.

'Certainly. One moment, there is a letter here marked for the "Attention of the Dean". He reaches into a shelf, takes out a letter and hands it over to the older man.

'Thank you.' He takes the letter.

'Pop the keys back to me when you've finished,' Robin says.

'Will do.'

As the pair walk inside I can hear that they are starting to argue again. 'I will make sure you don't do it,' the younger is saying in a seething voice as they set off through an archway.

The man called Robin turns to me. 'Yes, young man?' he says.

'I am coming here as a music scholar commencing in the Michaelmas term,' I tell him.

'Well, what can I do for you?'

'May I look around and acclimatise myself?'

'Go ahead.' 'Here, take this college guide book.' He hands it to me. 'Any questions just ask,' he smiles and adds, 'my name is Robin.'

'Yes I heard those men say your name,' I tell him. 'Was that the Dean just now?'

Robin nods. 'Yes, with an undergraduate. You'll be one of those next term.'

My heart does a jump of happiness as I walk through into an open grassed area. I hear music playing outside the chapel. On a notice board I read there is evening communion. It sends shivers of delight up my spine. I brush past a plant with yellow pom-pom flowers and the air becomes filled with the smell of spice. I enter the garden through the black painted wrought iron gates. The grass has been freshly mown. The atmosphere is serene.

Beyond the lawn is a set of about fifty steps. I refer to my guide book which tells me it is a burial mound for those who died in the Black Death. You can't imagine all those people suffering and dying today. Everything here is calm and peaceful. Death seems far away in this learned place.

I retrace my steps and enter the Cloisters. There is no-one else here. In the middle is grass and wooden seats. I sit on one which has a notice fixed to it saying it is donated by some farming tenants. A bell chimes and then I hear a piercing yell. It sounds like a person in agony.

A small speckled bird that was scratching around fallen leaves flies hastily away. The sound seems to have come from that tower. The bell tower says my guide book. On top are some stone figures. I refer to the guide book again. They represent seven virtue grotesques and their vices the gargoyles. The grotesques are ornate whilst the gargoyles have lead piping sticking out of their mouths. When the guttering is full of rain water it comes out through the gargoyles' mouths, the book says. I wish it was raining, so I can see this happen. It is not raining and my guide book says that this gargoyle represents Anger. Red starts coming out of the gargoyle's mouth; it looks like blood; surely it can't be blood.

I enter the chapel to find out where the red liquid is coming from. There, on my left, is a vast stained glass window depicting seven women. Above this stands a bearded man dressed in a robe, a mother and her babe lying in a wooden cot. The sunlight is streaming through, dancing beautiful colours across the marbled floor. I start to feel at peace again.

The service is still going on. I wonder if I should say something about the red stuff that looks like blood, but don't know who to tell. Anyway, I do not like to interrupt. I hear one of the priestly men say 'This is the body of Christ' and another adds, 'This is the blood of Christ.' Perhaps the red liquid is something to do with the service. I am still worrying about the red liquid coming out of Anger, though, and the way it happened so soon after that terrible shriek, when I see, coming out of a doorway at the side of the chapel, the young blonde undergraduate who had been walking with the Dean. What a relief, someone I recognise. I wonder where the Dean is. His cheeks are no longer ruddy, but are now very pale. The carnation he was wearing earlier has gone from his lapel.

'Excuse me,' I say. 'There is something like blood emerging out of the gargoyle representing Anger. Is that part of the service? Because it sounded like someone screaming just after I had looked up at the gargoyle.'

The undergraduate does not speak but looks at me. His eyes are cold. He does not answer. Keeping his gaze fixed on me; he raises his hand and combs it through his hair. When he takes his hand away his pale hair is smeared with red.

Access to New College is via New College Lane running into Queen's Lane. Was the red liquid part of the communion service or was it more sinister?

14

The Brewhouse Cats

NICHOLA MAY

As Margaret ripped off the final piece of parcel tape with a careless *whoop*, the slit of the box sprung open and she dived in. She emerged with small pieces of broken polystyrene hanging from her mousy perm and released the shrink-wrapped package with a pair of embroidery scissors.

This latest purchase had been a personal recommendation from Sandy. 'I got just a ting for your troubles Mrs Anderson,' Sandy had said after the second cup of tea. 'You the only one of my ladies who hasn't bought one.'

Last month 'just a ting' had been the ever-lasting nylon carpet anti-static device; the previous month it had been the tropical spider-displacer; and before then the simple pimple-extractor, the all-purpose metal handle degreaser, the ready-steady anyway-up household glove, and the under-shelf handy bottle top storage compartment. Margaret had lost count of all the objects that had been 'just a ting' for her troubles.

'This catalogue is the modern solution for the busy woman.' Sandy said. 'It is time, Mrs Anderson, for us women to rise up from our domestic chains and be free as the cat on the roofs.'

Sandy had first appeared in Paradise Square on a gloomy Tuesday back in February. Half way through a documentary about bubble wrap, Margaret had been interrupted by her *50-in-1 tunes* door bell and had opened the door to find a woman on the doorstep. The woman's shiny face was wound into a headscarf of such bright colours it looked as if she had been wrapped in a bunch of dahlias.

'My name,' the woman announced, 'is Sanura Butama. But my friends call me Sandy.' And with that a gust of wind inflated her unbuttoned coat and seemed to blow her into the hallway.

Sandy's voice was soft and musical and swept through the house like waves on a tropical beach. Her hair, released from the confines of the head scarf, took flight in twirls of delight as if dancing to some prohibited beat all of its own. Sandy's catalogue, full of items that Margaret had never seen or needed before, was irresistible.

The cat-scarer was bigger than Margaret expected. It was not, as she remembered from the catalogue, a sitting down cat; it was instead a ready-to-pounce cat, with two green translucent jewels for eyes and something at the back that resembled a battery pack.

But where to put it? None of the houses in Paradise Square had a back garden. In the end Margaret removed the broken plastic 'Santa Stop Here' sign from the planter by the front door and replaced it with the spike of the cat-scarer.

'What on earth do we want with that?' Kenneth said that night after they had gone to bed.

'Every one has one,' Margaret said, 'I thought you might be pleased.'

But Kenneth wasn't pleased. Kenneth was rarely pleased. He was eating a biscuit and now he brushed the crumbs across the bedcover onto Margaret's side.

Margaret rose and went to fetch the hand-held mini vac from last month's catalogue.

She stopped to look out of the window. From here she could see most of Paradise Square, which wasn't really a square at all, but rather an L-shaped road, sandwiched between two pubs and a tumble of garish red-brick flats built on the site where the brewery once was. The chimney of the brewhouse remained, but was trapped like some ancient relic inside a courtyard of flats. Another relic, the old brewery gate, gave the flats a deceptively grand entrance.

She saw that many of the houses along the square had cat scarers in their gardens now. The oriental-looking lady with four pretty daughters who lived next door had placed hers on the front lawn. It was the only lawn on Paradise Square.

The grey-haired arthritic Mrs Ballentino at no. 84 had put hers between her collection of ornamental hedgehogs and a cement rabbit. 'Indicative of the lower classes,' Kenneth had said when he first saw it.

At no. 78, the rental house, one of the students with long ginger hair and piercings had climbed out of a top window and fixed a cat-scarer onto the roof. It looked like a weather vane, thought Margaret. Kenneth had phoned the planning office to complain.

She went on standing at the window, looking out. The night was humid and breathless, the net curtains sucked in and out of the open bedroom window on imaginary air, bringing with them stagnant sounds from the street below.

She got back into bed at last, but in the early hours, when the heat was at its greatest, something startled her. Fully awake again, she lay listening. *The Jolly Farmers* would have shut its doors long ago; even the students next door would be in bed by now.

In the end she slipped out from under the covers,

stepped into her fawn slippers and white housecoat and went downstairs. She stood at the front doorstep, wishing she'd bought those Cool Air System Lounging Shoes from January's catalogue supplement.

There was a cat stretching the entire length of the concrete step and, at the sight of Margaret, it stood up, wound itself between her legs and gave out a sorrowful cry.

It looked hungry so she went into the kitchen, the cat following her, and took out the salmon she had set aside for Kenneth's supper. 'Well he can just do without can't he?' she said, scraping the fish into a china bowl. When the bowl was full she carried it outside and placed it on the front step, then stood watching while the cat ate Kenneth's meal. When the cat had finished, she reached towards its collar to see if there was some identification.

It was then that Margaret saw it.

Suspended on a ribbon from the cat's collar, and wrapped in almost translucent tissue paper, was a tiny box-shaped package. The corners were folded with such precision that it could have been wrapped by elves. Margaret ran her tongue along her lips and lifted her hand towards the collar. The cat retreated. Tail high and without looking back, it trotted into the darkness.

The following day Margaret hunted around Paradise Square, but there was no sign of the cat. Hoping it might return in the evening she ordered a crate of *Supreme Cat Food* and *Purrfect Nibbles.* She arranged the tins at the back of the cupboard where Kenneth wouldn't see them.

In the evening, as Margaret waited on the doorstep, the cat returned. As it devoured the meal Margaret surreptitiously tried to remove the package from its collar but at her touch the cat flinched and ran away.

The following evening, when the cat arrived, its fur was flattened with rain. The package, however, was as dry and perfect as the first evening Margaret had spotted it. Margaret presented the cat with a bowl of the expensive cat food and then waited. When there was nothing left but the soft crumbs of food on the cat's whiskers Margaret crept forward as if to stroke, then lunged. The cat leapt back with a screech. Its fur sprung into a mohican down the ridges of its spine and it took flight into the darkness.

Desperate and enraged, leaving the front door open, Margaret hitched up her housecoat with both hands and began to run down the street. Her fawn slippers slapped the tarmac, her fat knees tumbled past each other and the wild tail of her housecoat cord flew out behind her. At the end of Paradise Square, Margaret slipped and nearly tumbled into the weir but she had seen the cat. It was standing on the end of Quaking Bridge. She set off again in pursuit. The cat sped past the pub, down St Thomas' Street, turned its head then scampered down an entrance towards the flats.

'No!' Margaret sobbed. 'No! I *will* get you!' She took a sharp left after the cat and then skidded to a stop.

In the courtyard, beyond the brewery gate, 30 or more pairs of eyes were staring out at her. Moving. Blinking in synchronization. As if from one huge creature. There was not one cat, but many cats.

Margaret stepped under the ironwork arch of *The Lion Brewery* and through into the courtyard. There were cats of all sizes and types; a tiny Siamese-type cat with four pretty little kittens, a grey-haired cat with arthritic legs, a long-haired ginger cat with a spiky studded collar and many more.

The cat with the little package was there. It was watching her. She approached it. It did not run away. Her heart beating with anticipation she crouched down and ever so slowly slipped the package from its collar.

Margaret took the tiny box between finger and thumb. The sound of the millstream was roaring through her head. The cat watched her as she cupped the package in her hand, and then, barely breathing, she tugged at the ribbon. It came away in her hand so easily, so perfectly. The sheet of tissue paper released, melted into the rain, and the contents rolled into Margaret's palm. Her housecoat tail twitched. Then her lips parted and she let out a purr of delight.

When Kenneth woke up the next morning he was furious. His clothes weren't laid out, there was no breakfast and instead of his nicely prepared lunchbox, there were empty tins of cat food littering the draining board.

Angrily grabbing his coat at last, he marched out of the door, knocking an empty bowl off the doorstep, set off along the road, to work.

In the bedroom through a gap in the almost-closed curtains the morning sun was trying to break through.

A small beam of light bounced off the wall, illuminating a patch on the bed.

A white cat with fawn paws entered the room. It jumped up onto the bed and, lying in the sunlight, began licking biscuit crumbs from the covers.

The Brewery in St Thomas's Street dates from around 1782 and was owned by the Morrell family from the late 18th century until 1998.

Although the site was demolished in 2002 some of the original buildings remain, including the brewery offices (just inside the gate on the right), the yellow brick engine house, the chimney, and a waterwheel restored in 2003.

The brewery gate with its golden lions was designed in 1877 by local architect H. G. W. Drinkwater, who was also respons- ible for designing The Brewery Gate public house on St Thomas's street and several pubs and churches in the Oxford area. The name on the gate The Lion Brewery never gained popularity, and the brewery continued to be known as Morrells.

St Thomas's area has a long history of brewing dating back to the brew house of Oseney Abbey in the 15th century. The castle mill stream was chanelled from the Thames during medieval times and was vital for carrying goods through Oxford, includ- ing supplies of malt for brewing.

Quaking Bridge was originally a timber structure, dating from the 13th century or earlier. Canons of Oseney Abbey crossed over the bridge to perform services at the Chapel in the Castle. The present iron construction was erected in 1835.

15

The Explosion of Love

NEIL HANCOX

The red stain spattered her blouse and her ears were ringing. As she subsided into the chair she began to recall a clash of heads over forty years ago.

*

'Today', Jim Weller the science master, said, 'instead of class work we are going to visit Oxford's own Museum of the History of Science and see how some of Nature's secrets were prised from her grip'.

Thirty or so fifteen and sixteen year old pupils, sandwiched between the master and two burly prefects, trundled unwillingly down Broad Street. One or two muttered that it was probably better than hard benches in the science laboratory but most voted for boring as a better description.

Gordon Trickett, loitering towards the back, was indifferent. His main preoccupation was Beatrice Blackway, an angular girl with blond hair and heavy glasses, who had a most troubling effect on him. When he looked at her he was aware of the redness spreading across his face and drops of moisture forming on his upper lip. Beatrice, he knew, was unmoved. She followed Mr Weller's every word and had developed a sudden interest in chemistry. At the moment she was at the front of the group attempting small talk.

Gordon put his head down and pulled his frayed blazer close to his body to keep out the wind.

The woman at the entrance desk viewed the school party with suspicion. They were all potential vandals, particularly coming from *that* school.

'Downstairs first to the display of early scientific instruments', the master called out.

The room was filled with glass cabinets. Gordon counted about ten. Everything he could see was made from brass, with lenses added for microscopes and telescopes, and bits of wire for the electrical stuff. Occasionally decrepit notebooks, full of spidery writing and numbers, were placed next to an exhibit. Beatrice was listening intently and, no doubt, formulating an intelligent question.

He slipped a stick of gum into his mouth and sidled towards the exit. The nearby cabinet contained some old fashioned test tubes, a complicated bit of glassware labelled as a Liebig condensing column and one dusty glass bottle, with a rag on the top, containing a disgusting looking orange/brown liquid.

'I didn't know you were interested in chemistry, Trickett', the master said.

Gordon swallowed and saw Beatrice Blackway smirking at his embarrassment.

He attempted to speak but started coughing.

Beatrice intervened. 'Perhaps there is one of those metals that burn in water in that funny looking liquid, sir'? she suggested.

'No, Blackway. Metals burning in water – I expect you are thinking of metallic potassium. That has to be stored under paraffin oil. And potassium doesn't burn in water,' the master continued. 'The metal reacts with water and sufficient energy is generated to ignite the hydrogen produced.'

Beatrice reacted with enthusiasm. 'That's just what I meant, sir'. Gordon failed to see the difference.

He needed to get a better view of the bottle. As he tried to do so his head collided with Beatrice's blond curls.

'Ouch. Be careful,' she said without looking at him.

Gordon experienced a surge of excitement and thought that Beatrice may have coloured very slightly.

Later in the week the boy tackled his father.

'Dad, I think chemistry is interesting.'

His father, reading the evening paper, his tobacco-less pipe thrust firmly between yellowing teeth, considered the interruption. 'Is it, son?'

'Dad,' the boy continued, 'I'd like to go to university to study chemistry.'

His father shook his head. 'Get a trade son and don't fill your head with that nonsense.'

He returned to the evening's news in the *Oxford Mail*.

Gordon's mother overheard the conversation. She shaved part of her housekeeping allowance and bought her son a chemistry set.

The boy set to work at once. He dissolved, stirred, filtered, titrated and reacted.

'Copper sulphate has a lovely blue colour,' his mother observed.

One day at school Gordon heard a couple of sixth formers talking behind the bicycle sheds.

'You've got to mix sodium chlorate and a nitrate – can't remember which one. 'Then,' he continued, 'you stick in some . . .',

Gordon missed the details, 'and pack it into a tube and use a detonator.'

'That should make things go with a bang,' the second youth laughed.

The two boys suddenly turned round. 'Here, what are you staring at, Trickett? Push off.'

Gordon retired with a useful bit of information. It wasn't potassium in water on fire but it would make a bang and perhaps impress Beatrice Blackway, who seemed more unattainable than ever.

There was a tin of weed killer in his Dad's shed, with sodium chlorate on the label. The nitrate was the problem but eventually he found some in the school chemistry laboratory. 'It wasn't stealing,' he convinced himself. 'It was furthering his education.'

He mixed the two chemicals in a pudding basin and packed the result into a length of black plastic pipe. A detonator was more difficult until he remembered his cap gun. He put several caps between two hammer heads at the base of the plastic tube and banged the heads together.

'What the hell was that noise?' his father shouted. The shed window had shattered and Gordon emerged less his eyebrows. The boy knew his father's moods. This was the end of any university ambitions.

'You'll get two pounds fifty a week. Start on Monday.'

'What will I be doing Dad?' Gordon asked.

'Chemistry, bangs, all that stuff', his father said. 'It's

what you want. Down on the Osney Mead Trading Estate. It cost me several rounds at the local. So don't mess things up again. You'll pay your mother a pound a week for board and keep and get the shed window repaired.'

It would be good to have some money, Gordon thought. It would have been better going to university, though. He cheered himself up when he thought of Beatrice. He would ring up and ask her out.

'Hello Mrs Blackway, is Beatrice there?' Gordon said.

'No she is studying for her A levels and then she is going to university.' There was a pause. 'Goodbye Gordon.'

It was his first day. Gordon put on a clean shirt and a tie and was careful to be early. The laboratory manager eyed him morosely.

'Get rid of that tie,' he said. 'Safety hazard. Get a lab. coat and start washing that glassware. When you've done that clean up the bench. Just remember you are my assistant and there's a lot to learn.'

The boy looked around the grimy room. A fume cupboard, a Bunsen burner or two, a sink and rows of bottles. Not much scope for explosions here.

Gordon found the supply of dirty glassware unending. Anything interesting was always done by the manager, though most of the time he appeared to sit in his office with a half hidden copy of the *Racing Post*.

Twenty years later, Gordon's trousers had become tight. He loosened his belt. Too many burgers had done for his waistline what all those years of cleaning glassware and writing reports had done for his morale. Today, at least, would be different. His manager was leaving.

'Good luck Gordon. I've recommended that you take my place.' The man shook his hand.

Gordon surveyed his new responsibility. The poky little office was now his but not much else had changed over the years and he didn't even have an assistant.

*

Seventeen years passed.

'You've been with us, let me see, thirty-seven years Mr Trickett. Your influence on the company's reputation and input to its profitability, have been invaluable.'

It was a well tried formula that she delivered automatically, twisting a pencil between her fingers as she did so. A little too much pressure and the pencil shot out of her grasp and landed on the carpet. As she and Gordon both bent down to pick it up, their heads collided.

'Ouch.'

'Sorry.'

The woman addressing him no longer had blond hair, the angles had rounded with age, the glasses had gone and the surname was different. Underneath, he now knew, she had to be Beatrice Blackway.

The voice continued, 'So it seems fitting that you should enjoy the benefits of retirement while you can.'

Gordon gave her a big smile that started under his nose and went all the way to his ears. 'You don't believe that crap anymore than I do, Beatrice.' He emphasised the name. 'I've heard that they are outsourcing my services to Eastern Europe. Never mind,' he sighed. 'What's the offer?'

She was shaken. There was, she realised, something familiar about the man sitting opposite her and he knew her Christian name.

Slowly the scene came back to her. 'It's almost four decades, Gordon Trickett, since our heads clashed in the History of Science Museum. I've had one husband, deceased and two children, grown up. What about you?'

'Past president of the local model railway association, owner of a small detached house, garden shed in need of repair; company an old dog. Not what I imagined all those years ago, but I get by.'

'So, what is the offer?'

Beatrice slipped into automatic again. 'Enhanced pension up to the age of sixty, lump sum,'

'And,' Gordon chipped in, 'a gold watch?'

'Could be arranged,' Beatrice smiled.

'OK, I'll take it.'

He left her office. A career in chemistry, Gordon admitted, had been a big disappointment. Maybe Beatrice Blackway, husband deceased, still offered hope. Two pot noodles and a bottle of stout might do the trick. No, he had been living on his own for too long. Something more sophisticated – a decent restaurant, wine, and coffee afterwards at his place.

Gordon, in his best suit and a white shirt, nodded to the MD, Mr John Weller.

'Was your father a science master?' Gordon asked.

The MD was startled. 'Why yes, Mr Trockett.'

Human Resources, in the shape of Beatrice Blackway, whispered in the MD's ear, 'Trickett.'

'Yes, Mr Trickett, at a local school.'

'I thought so,' Gordon said. 'I was one of his pupils.'

'How interesting,' the MD replied hurriedly.

'Here's your long service watch, Donald.'

There was another fierce whisper, 'Gordon.'

Mr Weller now appeared thoroughly confused as to who was leaving. He presented the watch, with no words, simply a relieved smile.

Gordon thanked him and briefly took the extended hand.

Beatrice Blackway felt bad about the presentation. It was no way to treat staff, even those beyond their sell-by date. The MD might have more money but he lacked his father's charm. She walked over to Gordon. 'I do apologise,' she said, 'for the mix up with the names. It was really very unprofessional.'

As she was about to leave, Gordon touched her arm. 'Would you care to have dinner with me tonight? To celebrate my release.'

It was not, Gordon suspected, the sort of proposition she received very often, at least not from the past president of the local model railway association.

She hesitated. Gordon noticed the blush.

'Thank you Gordon. Unfortunately I have a meeting earlier. One I can't really avoid.'

Time to commit his reserves. 'How about a drink or coffee at my place afterwards?'

She surrendered. 'Than would be very pleasant, Gordon. I'll see you at nine thirty.'

'This is excellent wine, Gordon.'

He nodded. 'And I've something I want to show you.'

On the surface he was a quiet, middle aged man, Beatrice thought, and she was about to become a grandmother. What could this be?

Gordon had used his downstairs shower room as a

makeshift laboratory. He had carefully split a lump of potassium metal in two placing the smaller piece in a bottle of paraffin oil and sealing the remaining oil and metal in a freezer bag.

Now that it was time for the demonstration he began to panic. What if it didn't work? Or if Beatrice Blackway had forgotten?

As he reached for the small bottle his sleeve caught the freezer bag. It fell into the open toilet and, without thinking, Gordon pushed the 'full flush' button.

He ignored the diversion and took a couple of deep breaths to steady himself before he reappeared with a small dish filled with water. He placed this on the low table beside their wine and emptied the contents of the bottle into it. A pinpoint of silver flashed across the surface and burst into flames.

'Voila,' he exclaimed. 'I remember your interest in metals that burn in water from that school visit to the History of Science Museum all those years ago. I thought it might', he searched for a word,' well you might like to see it in action.'

As Beatrice smiled at the demonstration a hissing sound gathered in loudness and grew into a roar. Water, a smouldering towel and the remnants of a shattered toilet bowl erupted from the shower room into the hall.

Both of them jumped up, collided and knocked over the wine before beating out the flames. A shocked Beatrice noticed that her coat, draped over a chair, was soaking, charred and covered with pieces of porcelain, some of which bore unmistakeable signs of limescale.

There was wine on her blouse, her coat was ruined, the hall was a mess. She hoped that Gordon Trickett had an upstairs bathroom. He was an idiot, a menace. He was crazy. She should be furious and get out now. But he had remembered.

She looked at him sitting with his bright red face in his hands, staring. Beatrice sat down by him. 'I'll tell you a secret Gordon. I didn't like chemistry. It was the science teacher. I read psychology at university.'

They both started to laugh. She leaned across and kissed a hot, dishevelled, cheek.

Please note: under no circumstances should any of the experiments alluded to here be tried out. They can be very dangerous indeed.

The Oxford Museum of the History of Science is the oldest surviving purpose built museum for scientific instruments. The splendid building at the end of Broad Street originally housed the collection of Elias Ashmole.

Go inside and see the early electrical and optical instruments, often beautifully crafted from brass, devices used in past centuries for astronomical observations and surveying, some chemical apparatus and other curios. Then marvel at how some of Nature's secrets were extracted from her grasp using this quaint equipment. Without this basic information, painstakingly compiled over the years and centuries, there would be no modern science, communications, entertainment, computers and much more.

This wonderful source of knowledge is on your doorstep, in the centre of Oxford, and entrance is free! Go on, visit it.

16

Gargoyles

S. A. EDWARDS

The gargoyles that infested the buildings of Oxford were spreading, peering down from the roof tops and pulling faces. But they were the old ones. Too old to do her any harm. Their powers eroded.

But now new young ones had started creeping limpet-like down the buildings and were peeping into windows, watching her. They had started breeding, adapting and changing.

What would they do when they reached the ground? They wouldn't need to live on buildings any more.

She had seen them pretending to be ornaments, for God's sake, selling themselves in the tourist shops. They'd stuck themselves on to postcards. Is that how they were spreading? They were clever – she'd give them that.

Sitting in Café Loco on St Aldates, she ordered a coffee. The pretty Polish girl put it on the table.

'Are you OK? Is there a problem?' the girl asked gently.

She shook her head not lifting her eyes.

She knew there was one close, one low down, but she couldn't see it. When the waitress had gone she looked carefully around. She examined the ceiling, no gargoyles. Perhaps she was imagining it. Maybe it was just the gargoyles from Christ Church, the licheny bastards.

Then she saw it, pretending to be graffiti, spray painted on to a grey telecom box opposite the café window and low down almost at pavement level.

It caught her eye then looked away.

So that was their game.

Café Loco, The Old Palace, St Aldates. The café is located in a Grade 1 Sixteenth Century building. Graffiti on the telecom box located on Rose Street opposite the café windows may be by the elusive artist Banksy or may be worthless graffiti. You decide.

17

The Lily Pond

KAMINI KHANDURI

As the bells of Magdalen tower chimed the quarter hour, Alice pushed the palm house door shut behind her. She slumped back against the glass and a wave of humidity hit her like a slap in the face. She inhaled deeply, half intoxicated by the exotic scents. Overhead, the clear Oxford skies were masked by a canopy of lush green foliage. It was hard to believe that the Botanic Gardens were only metres away from the bustle of the High Street with its traffic and roadworks. But even in here, she couldn't escape. The voice of the man on the television came back to her: 'We will always remember her sparkling green eyes and her beautiful smile.' Beside him, his wife had sat motionless, her face drawn and grey, unable to look up at the flashing cameras. The grieving pair. The parents of the dead girl. Alice shook herself. She had to stop dwelling on it. After all, it might never have happened.

She wandered, lost in the tropical paradise. Her shoulders loosened and her mouth relaxed into a smile. She began to feel peaceful. If there was anywhere she'd be able to forget, it would be here. She stroked the rough trunk of the cocoa tree and ran her fingers up and down the tall multi-sectioned stems of a sugar cane plant. Perhaps she should tell someone. But what would she say? Nestling at the foot of the trees were clumps of red fly agaric mushrooms with their white-spotted tops. The label said that they had hallucinogenic properties. 'She was only seventeen,' the girl's father had said. Seventeen. Too young to die. How unfair that all these plants were thriving when the poor girl's life had been cut short. Alice's eyes prickled with tears. She stumbled past the cotton plant with its fluffy white balls and the rosy periwinkle, which, so the label said, produced chemicals that helped cure leukaemia. The blackbirds outside warbled and the leaves rustled soothingly, like a sigh, almost like a whisper . . . Was that a whisper? She looked round but no one was there. It must have been the ferns moving as she brushed past.

The path led to the lily pond. Out of breath, Alice rested against the rocky edge and watched the tadpoles and tiny fish darting in the murky water. Her stomach was churning and her hands were sticky with sweat. When she closed her eyes, she could see the girl's mother's accusing face.

Around the pond grew water lettuce, rice plants and papyrus. There were banana plants, their ridged leaves stretching up to the sun. And the lilies themselves – huge flat pads sitting on the pond's surface. Some smooth, some spiky, some small and some as large as dinner plates. *'Victoriana cruziana'* Alice read on one label. With a perfect lip around its edge, it resembled an over-sized pie dish and was apparently strong enough to hold the weight of a child. The exquisite flowers were splashes of colour scattered around the pond. There were delicate white flowers, their partly-closed petals curving upwards into a point. Creamy yellow flowers like giant buttercups. And deep purple flowers with spiky pink-tipped petals and golden centres. The pineapple-sweet fragrance of the lilies filled Alice's nostrils. She began to feel hopeful. Everything would be all right.

And again, there was the whispering. She spun round. Was someone playing tricks? But no one was there.

'For God's sake Alice, get a grip. Now you're imagining things,' she muttered to herself as she moved away from the pond. *Alice* – it came again. She froze. It must be the leaves. Her heart was beating fast. It was too hot, she decided. She'd go and cool down in the alpine house. As she retraced her steps she couldn't help noticing that the path was made of hardened mud.

'That's strange,' she thought, 'I'm sure it used to be wooden decking? Anyway, the door's just round this next bend.' But it wasn't. The path meandered on, but no door appeared. And now she couldn't see any glass walls. Just thick foliage. No glasshouse roof, its panes criss-crossed with metal frames. Just the huge curving branches, and beyond them endless blue sky. A shiver ran down her spine and she felt panic. Where the hell was the exit? She started to hurry. *Alice! Alice!* It sounded closer now. The hairs on her arms were standing up. 'Who's there?' she called.

She began to run. 'Is anyone there?' she shouted. But no one answered. And now she was crying, her legs felt weak, her head was spinning. The strong scents of the tropical plants, which only a while ago had helped her relax, were now overpowering and unbearably sickly. She stumbled and fell, crawled under some branches and collapsed on the soil, leaning back against the comforting firmness of a gnarled tree trunk. Instead of the blackbird's song, she could hear parrots squawking, cicadas chirping, and monkeys chattering. The father's voice was ringing in her ears: 'Nothing will bring her back . . .We'd like to appeal to the driver . . .'

She had been driving along the ring road, Elgar's cello concerto blasting from the CD player. It was midnight on a cool clear evening and the roads were empty. They'd just had the biggest row of their entire marriage. In the end, she'd snapped. Draining her glass of wine, she smashed it to the floor, watched it splinter into fragments and slammed out of the house. As she drove away, she opened her mouth and let out a deeply satisfying roar.

Now in the glasshouse, it seemed to be getting dark and the heat was stifling. The sound of the monkeys was louder and she could hear something large moving through the foliage. She swallowed with fear. Her mouth was full of saliva but her throat was dry. 'Water!' she gasped. 'I need water.'

She knew she was breaking the speed limit, but who was there to see? A group of people was crossing the road ahead. They were some distance away and without needing to touch the brake, she watched them safely reach the opposite side. She congratulated herself on her sound judgement despite having had a few drinks.

Staggering to her feet, she followed the path until she found herself back at the lily pond. Relieved to see a familiar landmark, she sank to her knees at the pond's edge and dipped her hands in the water. Tepid rather than cold, it was still refreshing and she plunged her arms in up to the elbows.

The music soared as it reached a climax. She sang along and put her foot down, enjoying her control of the vehicle. Then a shape appeared as if from nowhere. A shape in the road, moving from side to side. Was it a person? Was she just imagining it?

Alice lifted her arms from the water and breathed slowly, trying to calm herself. 'A girl of seventeen has been killed by a hit-and-run driver,' the newscaster had said. Alice pressed her hands over her ears. Her face was burning hot.

Feeling confused, she slammed on the brake. The car started to slow but it was too late. There was a dull thud as she hit something. A person? Or just a branch from an overhanging tree. Or maybe an animal – a fox or a deer? She'd been driving too fast. And she'd had too much to drink.

Leaning over the pond, she closed her eyes and splashed the soothing water onto her cheeks. And then it came again. *Alice. Alice.* But this time it was different. More like a gurgle than a whisper or a sigh. As if it was underwater. Frozen with fear, Alice opened her eyes. And there, centimetres away from her, just under the surface of the water, was a face. The face of a young girl with green eyes.

Take a stroll up High Street to find a few moments of peace in a busy city. Beyond Queen's Lane but just before Magdalen Bridge you'll find Oxford's Botanic Gardens. The garden was founded

in 1621 on the banks of the River Cherwell in the corner of Christ Church Meadow. It stands on land that was once a Jewish cemetery. It's the oldest botanic garden in Britain, one of the oldest scientific gardens in the world, and is home to 7,000 different types of plant – though they're not all on display. There's more biological diversity here than there is in a tropical rainforest! Visit the glasshouses and marvel at the giant lilies in the Lily House, search for cocoa, oranges, pawpaws and coconuts in the tropical Palm House, or escape to the desert in the Cactus House. Then wander in the walled garden and have a look for the oldest tree – the English yew planted by the garden's first curator, Jacob Bobart, in 1645. Can you find the black pine tree, now one of the largest trees in the garden? This tree has been the inspiration for many writers, from J. R. R. Tolkien to Philip Pullman. And Lewis Carroll, the Oxford mathematics professor who wrote Alice's Adventures in Wonderland, was a frequent visitor in the 1860s. In fact, you can see the dome of the Lily House in the background of one of Tenniel's classic illustrations for Carroll's book.

18

Florence Park

SABITA BANERJI

Florence has been dancing
It's her final fatal fling
Before the winter comes to silence her
And close her spirits in.

She's dyed her hair bright auburn
Thrown off her sober greens
To dress in daring reds and lemon yellow.
She's drenched herself in gold

In brass and copper bangles
Which jangle when she snaps
Her thin black fingers.

Her gorgeous gowns are slipping, now
Exposing skinny shoulders
And her many rosy nipples
To the ice blue sky.

But this doesn't trouble Florence,
Whose mulberry lips
Blow you sweetly sticky kisses
As you pass her by.

Florence has been dancing
And she doesn't care who knows it.
She's dyed her hair bright auburn
And the wicked wind blows it.
The wind has torn her dress off
And scattered all her baubles
On the ground.

Florence stands there naked
And the wind sighs through her ribs
With something like regret.
Her spirit has retreated
Six feet under.

In the moist dark heart
Of her bed her spirit's sleeping
Remembering the glory
Of her final, fatal fling

But soon her nerves are tingling
With sweet anticipation
Of the orgy that she's going to throw in Spring!

Florence Park is in East Oxford between Iffley Road and Rymers Lane. The main entrance is from Florence Park Road.

19

In Memory of Comets

JANET BOLAM

'Mum, is Joe eating with us tonight?'

'Yes, and before you find an excuse not to be there, remember the pocket money deal.'

Susan watched her daughter as she debated between sharing a meal with Joe and the prospect of enough money to buy a pretty top she'd seen. It was worth one more try.

'But I feel sick and I'll puke up all over the table if I have to watch him eating, I know I will.'

Susan settled her eye on her 13 year old daughter and thrust some plates into her hand.

'Set the table and shut up.'

Every week it was the same. Joe had started to come to dinner once a week in the early post operative days when he found it difficult to adjust to life with one leg. Now he was managing very well, but the habit of the weekly meal was firmly established in his mind, so every Monday he would call to confirm that he was expected and every week Susan and Mandy argued about it.

It was generally acknowledged that Joe was amazing for his age. Even though he only had one leg, he refused a wheelchair, preferring to walk with a false leg. He lived alone in his own ground floor flat. There was little that did not interest him. His visits were peppered with eager questions and debate on topics as varied as the politics of the day (too right wing), the latest play at the Playhouse (he preferred the classics), and his beloved music. He still played his violin in a small quartet and after dinner he would frequently play the piano for the family, loosely banging out chords, singing Gershwin and Sondheim, much to Mandy's distress.

His taxi drew up into the drive.

Davy viewed 'Joe evenings' with great delight. It was Davy who first called him Gungy Joe. This referred to the drifts of dandruff mixed liberally with clippings from his beard that permanently coated his shoulders and rolled down his food stained shirt.

'So kind, so kind.' Joe wobbled his way into the living room. He was still a little unstable, tending to stop and sway dramatically at regular intervals. ' I've brought you a present. Some homemade yoghurt with garlic.' He indicated a grubby plastic bag tied onto his stick. Susan carefully extracted it and helped Joe to a seat.

'Mandy loves your homemade yoghurt.' With an evil leer Davy took the grey leaking jar from the bag and waved it in front of his sister's face. Mandy, who had been trying not to breathe through her nose since Joe's arrival managed a smile.

'How nice and thoughtful of you Joe.' Susan took the jar away into the kitchen followed closely by Mandy

'Mum' she whispered urgently 'He absolutely stinks.'

'Yes, it does seem a bit worse than usual,' Susan agreed.

'A bit! I can't bear it. You're not putting that stuff into the fridge are you?'

'Just until he goes home. A mark of respect.'

Conversation around the table was lively. Davy was learning about comets at school and it had caught his imagination. This was no surprise since the comet Hale Bopp had been making spectacular appearances in the night sky for the past 3 months.

'Isn't that the one that was discovered by Halley?' ventured Susan

'Oh Mum! That's Halley's comet, not Hale-Bopp. I can't believe you thought that!' Sometimes Mandy found lesser mortals trying, especially her mother.

'I remember my mother told me she saw Halley's comet

when she was a girl. There were no electric street lights in those days, so it could be seen very clearly. She told me that she agreed to marry my father the day she saw it. Fireworks.' Joe pierced a pea that flew to the ground to join the rest of the food scattered around his feet.

'Halley's comet came in 1910 then 1986 and it's going to come again in 2061.' Davy was a mine of information. 'When we go on our school trip, we're going to see the house he lived in. There's an Observatory on the top. Halley was the one who discovered that it was the same one coming back and back and back. . . .'

'What school trip?' Susan realised she had not mined Davy's school bag for notes from school for quite some time.

'The one I've been telling you about. I bet you don't know the difference between a comet and an asteroid, Mandy.'

'Why would I care? 'Mandy was edging towards the door.

'Comets have tails and asteroids don't! What do you think the tail is made of?'

'I read an advertisement for plane rides.' Joe helped himself to more potatoes 'You can hire them at Kidling-ton Airport and they take you up at night so that you can see the comet clearly. We would be above all the electric lights and see it just like my mother and father did.'

'But it's not the same comet. . . .' Mandy started, but caught Susan's eye and held her tongue.

'Yes, it would be magical to do that.' Joe blinked behind his glasses 'Wonderful potatoes, Susan. I don't suppose I could interest any of you in a plane ride?'

The small plane sat on the airfield, the engine running. Joe slowly crossed the tarmac with Susan anxiously holding his elbow to prevent him falling. Davy was already mounting the steps onto the plane. He could hardly contain himself. 'Can I sit next to the pilot? Do you think we will see the edge of the Milky Way? Will we be able to see the Comet's tail?' At 4000 feet above Oxfordshire, the plane turned north. The Pilot could be heard over the headphones.

'A good night for comet watching,' he was saying. 'We will soon see Banbury.'

'You look very pale darling,' Susan noticed her daughter was clutching her middle. 'Are you OK?'

'I feel sick.' She leaned forward, grabbed a paper bag and retched. Meanwhile Joe, who had been staring intently out of his window, let out a long, low fart. Mandy vomited.

'This is the best view I have ever seen of the comet!' The pilot continued unaware of the visceral drama being enacted in the passenger compartment. 'Those of you on the left-hand side can see it now.'

Craning her neck, Susan stared hopefully into the heavens. Joe had his handkerchief out and was alternating attempts to clean the window with bashing his glasses as he pushed his head next to the thick glass. The stars were bright pinpoints on a black velvet sky. 'Do you think that's the comet?' Susan and Mandy stared doubtfully at Venus. 'No, but aren't the stars amazing? Even if we don't see the comet, it's worth it.'

Mandy smiled.

'Beautiful clarity tonight' the pilot said. 'One more time around and then we must prepare for landing.'

Joe banged his walking stick on the glass furiously. The comet appeared to be hovering right outside his window, like a visiting Greek god. Surreal, large and bright with its tail divided into two fins, it was perfectly framed by the window.

They watched, transfixed until the plane turned and it disappeared from view.

On the way home in the taxi, Davy slept between Susan and Mandy. Joe sat in the front seat, smiling as he remembered his Mother's face, animated as she described the incredible day she saw Halley's comet.

In memory of Fred Porter, who was a dear friend.

Edmund Halley (1656–1742) was an English astronomer and mathematician who was the first to calculate the orbit of the comet later named after him. While in Oxford, he attended The Queen's College and lived in a modest white house, near the Bridge of Sighs on New College Lane, which also accommodated his Observatory. A plaque, just visible through the bushes, marks the spot. The range of Halley's scientific interests was enormous: he did work on the variation of the earth's magnetic field, the variation of barometric pressure with height, the salinity and evaporation of oceans, and the optics of the rainbow. He also translated the geometrical works of Apollonius and even reconstructed a missing section. Without him, Newton's Principia would not have existed, for it was Halley who pressed Newton to publish and who paid for the printing himself.

In 1703 Halley was elected to the Savilian Chair of Geometry at Oxford and ended his career as Astronomer Royal. He died in 1742 after drinking a glass of wine against his doctor's orders. He was eighty-six.

20

Lost and Found

VICKY MANCUSO BREHM

Charlotte followed the others into the silent college chapel with its high ceilings and rich wood panelling. There was a smell of musty hymn books. It was smaller, less grand, more intimate than the numerous other chapels the group had already been taken to. It made Charlotte feel at home.

In the background the tour guide's voice was like the roar of distant traffic, explaining the college's literary connections.

'. . . and William Tyndale, who courageously translated the Bible into English back in the sixteenth century, was one of the College's most famous alumni. Now I would like to move on fairly promptly to our next college, Magdalen. We will spend longer there, given its association with C. S. Lewis. Follow me everyone.'

The group was leaving. As Charlotte headed towards the door she noticed an unusual stained glass panel against

the back wall of the chapel. It was illuminated from behind
and portrayed a ponderous man wearing Tudor dress.
Although the panel was traditional in its style, it looked
new. A black and white cat was curled up asleep on a chair
next to it, cosy on a soft cushion.

Outside in the summer sun the others were already
leaving the quad. 'Why is the guide always in such a
rush?' sighed Charlotte. That was the problem with the
tour; there was no time to stop and enjoy the sights. The
tour that in the brochure had sounded so appealing,
consisted, instead, of ten days on a cramped coach, and
rushing from sight to sight. Charlotte's blisters growing
more painful by the day.

Derek had insisted that she should go without him.
Charlotte wished he had wanted to come. She had gone,
instead with her friend, Connie.

When Charlotte caught up with the group, they were
just leaving Hertford College through the disproportio-
nately large wooden doors. They turned right opposite the
Bodleian Library, then right again towards the Bridge of
Sighs where they stopped briefly to take photos. Charlotte
reached into her handbag to take out her camera. It wasn't
there.

'Connie,' Charlotte sighed, 'I must have left my camera
in the college chapel . . . I'll have to go back for it.'

'The guide won't be pleased – there is no way she is going to wait for you. Why don't you meet us there?' suggested Connie, who was used to her friend's scatty ways. 'Make sure you keep your mobile on in case you get lost.'

Charlotte retraced her steps feeling a sudden relief at breaking free. She walked slowly. The giant blue cupola of the Radcliffe Camera glimmered majestically in the distance.

Back at Hertford, the soft green carpet of lawn shimmered in the July sunshine, the creepers on the buildings were vibrant as emeralds against the honey-coloured stone. Charlotte walked self-consciously past a group of people near the chapel entrance. Inside the chapel, she had a quick hunt around and found her camera next to the mysterious panel. The blisters on her feet were so sore. She sat down on one of the long wooden benches, relieved by the cool quietness, her mind swirling in a mixture of thoughts and prayers.

The black and white cat, now awake, tiptoed towards her meowing. It purred as she stroked its head.

'Hello pussy,' she said. The cat jumped up on to her lap. The two sat quietly like old friends. A moment of quiet after ten days of madness. A moment of perfect bliss.

Eventually the cat jumped down and trotted towards the door. Charlotte did not know how long she had been sitting there, but acknowledged reluctantly that it must be time to join the others. She followed the cat past the glass panel and out of the chapel. As she stepped out into the quad, her stomach churned with panic as she realised she had no idea which college they were going to next. What had the guide said? Was it Merton, or was that where they had been that morning? She vaguely recalled a mention of C. S. Lewis.

The cat stood next to her, rubbing its head against her leg. She looked up to see two women making their way towards her.

'Hello Simpkins!' said one of the women, smartly dressed and in her late twenties. She bent down to stroke her feline friend.

A waiter carrying a tray with drinks was coming towards them.

'Would you like some sherry?' he asked Charlotte.

'Oh! No thanks. I . . .' she hesitated for a moment.

'Would you prefer Pimms and lemonade?' enquired the waiter.

Pimms and lemonade sounded perfect in this beautiful place. Perhaps it was a thirst for freedom after ten days of being hostage to The Tour. Probably, it was because Derek was not there. He would have said 'No thanks, I am not with this group.'

'Yes please,' Charlotte heard herself say. The waiter handed her a fluted champagne glass full of a sparkling drink the colour of diluted caramel. She took a sip, tasting summer, garden parties and fruit.

The two young women re-surfaced from their conversation with Simpkins and both accepted drinks too.

'Hi. I'm Louise and this is Anne. We studied History from '95 to '98,' explained Louise.

'I'm Charlotte. Where are you from?'

The two friends told Charlotte they had travelled from London for the day, where Louise worked as a lawyer. Anne had a job in marketing. They chatted for a while. Young, professional women living in London; they seemed to Charlotte like an exotic species. They were so different from Charlotte's friends back home who were middle-aged, predictable and safe, concerned with their kids and their ageing parents.

A smartly-dressed older man came over to introduce himself.

'I'm the new Principal, Roger Cornby-White.' His public school voice boomed out like a foghorn. He shook Charlotte's hand, rattling the bones in her arm. He had the beaming smile of a natural host, oozing confidence.

'I'm Charlotte, Charlotte Johnson.'

'Ah, one of our American friends! What did you study?'

'English.' Charlotte replied, convincing herself that it was not a lie. She had indeed studied English. At Iowa State University.

'English, excellent! There are a group of English graduates talking to Dr. Foster over there. I will make sure I introduce them to you at lunch.'

'Oh no,' Charlotte interjected, alarmed, 'I am not staying for lunch.'

'Nonsense, you must join us since you have come all this way.'

'No but . . .'

'I insist.'

'But you see I didn't . . .'

'I will have a word with the catering manager, I am sure they can squeeze in one more place.' And with that he marched off.

Charlotte stood, mouth open. What should she do? She could – and of course should – just leave. Or she could sit quietly at a table and be served lunch. She looked at what she was wearing. Apart from her sensible shoes, she was not exactly under-dressed; maybe she could get away with it.

The moment of decision crept up faster than she was expecting. The foghorn voice of the Principal was announcing that lunch was being served in the dining hall. People started to file past her to the far side of the quad.

They were heading for an extraordinary building. It looked like a circular staircase with windows following the curve of the stairs. The parallel rows of glass circled upwards like the stripes on a candy cane. Charlotte had decided. She set off with the crowd.

She circled giddily up the worn grey steps and into the oak-panelled dining hall. Three rows of tables the length of the hall were set for lunch, each place setting having a dizzying array of cutlery and a sparkling collection of glasses of different sizes. At the opposite end of the room was a perpendicular high table on a raised platform.

Another moment of panic: where should she sit?

'Come and sit with us,' offered Anne and Louise, sensing her hesitation.

'Thank you.' Charlotte shuffled behind them, her cheeks flushing as the reality of her deceit began to sink in.

She sat with Anne on one side and John, who had studied PPE, whatever that might be, on the other.

'Where are you from?' asked John.

'Iowa.'

'Did you see the article about Tyndale in *The Economist* a few months ago?'

Charlotte was speechless for a moment. 'No, I don't keep up with Hollywood that much,' she replied at last. John stared at her. Oh no, what had she said? Tyndale, why was the name so familiar?

'Yes, I read it,' Anne volunteered. 'I thought it was interesting how they compared Tyndale to modern-day political dissidents. An interesting theory, though stretching the facts somewhat.'

'Absolutely,' said John, giving up on Charlotte. 'Tyndale was not interested in politics. He did not set out to get into trouble with the authorities, that was just a consequence of his work.'

'Yes, and it was good to see him being given credit for his contribution to the development of the English language.'

'And it must have taken some perseverance to carry on with the work when he was receiving no credit for it, in fact quite the opposite,' continued John.

A waiter placed an elegantly arranged plate of melon and port before Charlotte. It was delicious. John and Anne discussed Tyndale, then drifted into some detailed discussion on human rights issues and the role of the International Criminal Court in The Hague.

Charlotte sat back and enjoyed the conversation, the atmosphere, the jokes and the waiter-service. She felt relaxed. Maybe it was the Pimms. Maybe it was just this deep yet ridiculous sense of feeling that she fitted in. Her life back home, the suburban house, the double garage, the housework, teaching Dickens to her disinterested pupils, seemed so bland. Of course she loved everyone back home. But this was exciting; eating a three-course meal in the middle of the day, talking of politics and literature, meeting these people from a different world. She wished she were twenty again.

The main course of roast duck was served. Charlotte had not eaten duck before; it tasted good.

'Ladies and Gentlemen,' broke forth the voice of the Principal standing up to give a speech as dessert was being served.

'Let me welcome you back to the College, on this auspicious occasion, the dedication of the Tyndale panel in the College Chapel. We are honouring one of the College's most famous alumni today for his courage and conviction, which he paid for with his life.'

The Principal paused, his strong face suddenly serious.

'We are pleased to commemorate his bravery with the new stained-glass panel in the Chapel. Thank you each and every one for your generous contributions.' The audience applauded. The Principal went on to explain the process of commissioning and installing the panel, before proposing a toast.

'To William Tyndale and the Hertford Alumni Association.' Everyone in the hall rose and raised their glasses in a toast.

When lunch was over, people started to drift reluctantly out of the hall, condensing years of their lives into tiny fragments of conversation. Charlotte followed the crowd down the circular staircase and out into the bright sunshine and gaudy green of the quad.

The Principal approached her.

'Have you seen the Tyndale panel yet?'

'Why, I don't think so,' Charlotte replied, unsure. Uncertainty was the wrong approach to take with the Principal.

'Let me show you before you go.' He led her into the chapel and pointed to the glass panel that Charlotte had seen earlier.

'I think it is very fitting.' The Principal sounded like a proud father. Simpkins was back on his chair next to the panel, fast asleep.

After a few minutes admiring the panel, the Principal turned to say goodbye.

'Lovely to see you. You must come to another reunion next time you are over,' said the Principal, shaking her hand.

Standing next to the portrait of a man of such integrity was making Charlotte feel uncomfortable. Her conscience was running on overtime under Tyndale's steady gaze.

'I'm afraid there has been a misunderstanding.' The words seemed to be making their own way out of her mouth.

'Oh?'

'You see, I didn't study English here at all. I studied at Iowa State University. I tried to explain . . . I am so sorry about lunch, I will settle up with the College . . .'

'Oh! You mean I dragged you up to lunch . . .' The Principal stared at her motionless. 'No, it is I who must apologise,' he said. 'My wife says I never listen to anyone. Yes, I recall now, you did try to tell me you weren't staying for lunch. So what brought you to Hertford?'

Charlotte felt her cheeks warming. 'I have come on a literary tour of Oxford.'

'A tour? You mean you are a tourist?'

Principal Cornby-White roared with laughter. 'You must come again! Why you are practically an honorary member now!'

Charlotte looked up at the portrait. It seemed that even Tyndale had a smile on his face.

Nestling opposite the Bodleian Library on Catte Street, little Hertford College traces its origins to Elias de Hertford's Hart Hall, founded in the late thirteenth century. It was upgraded to Hertford College in 1874, thanks to its benefactor the financier Sir Thomas Baring. In the following fifty years, the College was rebuilt and gained some architectural gems, such as its Hall with its unusual spiral staircase and the iconic bridge over the New College Lane that joins two of the College's quads.

William Tyndale studied at the then Hart Hall in the sixteenth century at the height of the Reformation. Tyndale spent his life translating the Bible into English, but did not live to see his work completed. Condemned as a heretic, after years spent in hiding he was eventually martyred in Brussels in 1536. Nevertheless Tyndale's translation formed the basis of the first New Testament in English and later the complete Bible in English, printed very shortly after his death.

The commemorative stained glass panel depicting Tyndale is on display in Hertford College's chapel. The spiral staircase and dining hall where Charlotte had lunch are on the left as you come into Hertford's main quad. Both can be accessed through the College's main entrance on Catte Street.

21

Manuscript

KATHLEEN DALY

Welcome to my world. Perhaps you have come half-way across the globe to see me. Perhaps you have come across the street. I have been entombed in my box in the dim recesses of the library stacks. I have been waiting for you.

What will I be to you? You brush past the custodian, you seize me with a curt nod, you deposit me on the desk, rifle my contents, discard me. I shall be a mere footnote in your learned tome.

You, though, you enter silently, awed by the vacant spaces. Your eyes glide over the painted page of the ceiling to the splintered colours of the Selden End. You spy out the carols where so many eminent scholars have worked. You watch the Librarian unlock the wooden fortress enclosing Bodley's most precious manuscripts. You cradle me in your arms, you pose me on the foam lectern. You caress my crimson binding. You stroke the smooth flesh of my ivory leaves, the fine black follicles from corpses that went to create me. You devour my fluid script, the yellow flush of my majuscules, you savour the azure, the mallow, the burnished gold of my initials, the breast of a letter where a bee sits, its folded wings filmy and transparent. I am the key to your work, the evidence you have been searching for all your life, your illumination.

Feast on my intricate borders of lapis, scarlet, viridian. Birds swoop through ivy and acanthus leaves, dive among violets, strawberries and columbines. A cat claws their plumage. A monkey plays a pipe and tabor. Urns overflow with flowers. A monk bestrides a hobby horse. A child snares a rabbit in his hood.

Move beyond the frame. Glance through the open windows, at my landscapes. A peasant and his donkey cross the fields. A boat with its angler floats along a river, a watermill churns the current. Swans glide over a mirror lake. A shepherd herds sheep, while his wife gently guides them into a wattle pen. Knights ride towards the turrets of distant castles. City walls melt into a blue haze. Ships unfurl their sails on faraway seas. Rays of sun stream down from heaven like a benediction.

Look again at the foreground. Armies are locked in combat, death contorts the bodies of men and horses. This is the land of the Apocalypse, of war, famine, sickness, and death. Brothers turn against fathers. Invaders sweep across France. Cities are starved and looted, the countryside is laid waste. Inside my pages, my creators wage war.

My artist learned his trade in enemy territory. He was a collaborator's apprentice. While his Master painted the foreground of a scene, he drew the landscapes. How he yearns for those days, as his eyes turn to glass and his apprentices snigger at the old-fashioned images they copy from his pattern books.

My author is a patriot, whose book must be fit for the king he followed into exile. He orders my artist to paint the major figures, he doesn't want an apprentice foisted on him. He pays for the best pigments. But pictures themselves have no beauty or meaning. Only words count.

My artist hates my author, that tormentor, that clanging cymbal, though he cannot afford to turn away his business. My craftsman sees each picture as a web of illusion, of shape and pattern, light and shade, space and volume, where colours collide and separate, oppose and complement each other.

Reach into the picture. Feel the texture of velvet and silk and fine wool under your hand, the cold glaze of tiles under your feet. Step into this image. Watch blood vibrating in veins, spilling from wounds, hear laughter and cries of anguish. Inhale breath scented with cinnamon and cloves, the smoke of burning buildings, the odour of decay. Follow the path winding across the landscape. Run your hand up the bark of the tree. Grasp at the leather suspended over your head. Listen to the rope creaking in the breeze.

And when you have done shuddering, when you have run back the way you have come, scattering the sheep, astonishing the shepherd, when the knights have parted before your headlong flight, stretch out your hands and claw at the picture plane. Thrust back your chair. Rush from the library. Who will see your empty eyes? Who will notice one more figure in the landscape? The last scholar miscounted, it happens to the best of them. And I shall wait for my next reader.

Duke Humfrey's Library was constructed in the late fifteenth and seventeenth centuries and is part of the Old Bodleian Library (between Broad Street and Radcliffe Square). This story was inspired by the 'Historical Mirror of France' (MS Bodley 968) made in France at the end of the Hundred Years War (c.1451), and its fifteen fine illustrations. The manuscript is not on public display but there are regular guided tours of the

Bodleian Library that include a visit to Duke Humfrey's Library. The rest is fiction: to the author's knowledge, no book in the Bodleian has ever devoured its reader.